Barnsley

GO

P.S

Family Missing

Gail Jones

Published in 2012 by FeedARead.com Publishing –
Arts Council funded

A CIP catalogue record for this title is available from
the British Library.

Praise for Gail Jones

Family Secrets

A heart warming and realistic story, once I started I couldn't put it down. Ideal book for 12+.'   Melissa

'Family Secrets' is a really imaginative and eventful book. It's absolutely great for teenagers. Especially because of the emotions and how realistic the characters are! Jade yr7

I think 'Family Secrets' really inspired never to get upset about bullies and never punch them in the nose.' Joseph aged 11

Family Fear

This is an enthralling storyline and the way the writer captures the personality of the characters is amazing. Once I started reading I couldn't put the book down.   Christina – 12-year-old bookworm!

A great read. Inspiring and heart warming with the occasional disaster! A real page turner, highly recommended! Naomi (adult)

Can't wait for 'Family Missing' to come out, I've read 'Family Fear' and 'Family Secrets'!! Best books I've read, :) Sophie aged 11

Family Missing

Great story with plenty of suspense. Ellen aged 15

The book was really cool. It's a whirlpool of adventures going on all over the place. Hania aged 13

After enjoying books 1 and 2 this was like sitting down with old friends, couldn't put it down until I had finished reading it. Pam (adult)

THE STORY SO FAR

*Hi, I'm Rachel and I'm fifteen-years-old. These last twelve months have been the hardest of my life. So much has happened that I've already filled two books -'**Family Secrets**' and '**Family Fear**'.*

Anyway, for anybody who hasn't read those I'll give you a quick update so you'll know what's been going on.

Back in February, Dad got a new job and moved us from Scarborough, a lovely sea side town to Rotherham in South Yorkshire. There's a few parks around here and a big shopping centre called Meadowhall not far away but definitely no sea.

With my gran and all my friends back in Scarborough I had to start all over again. When small but confident Emma befriended me on my first day I thought I was so lucky. She seemed great at first but then she saw me smiling at Luke, who is now my boyfriend, she flipped her lid because she fancied him. Turns out Emma likes all her own way and if she doesn't get it she tries to destroy the person who crosses her. Her dad's this ace reporter and he finds

5

out all sorts of stuff but he's a nice guy and doesn't print anything harmful. (I know, unusual for a journalist). Unfortunately Emma is nothing like him. She listens in on his conversations and snoops in his office. She even does her own research then uses what she finds to make everybody at school do what she wants.

Well, she'd overheard her dad saying he'd recognised mine when he came to collect me from their house one day. He remembered my dad adopting this one-year-old girl who'd been found abandoned at just a couple of weeks old. Bet you can guess who that was. Well, I knew nothing about this and Emma took great pleasure in breaking the news to me in front of my whole class.

I didn't believe her, of course, but later when I asked Mum and Dad they confirmed it. To say I was devastated would be like saying supermodels are a bit thin. I was a complete mess and it didn't help that my (adoptive) parents were obviously keeping something else from me as well.

I decided to find out what it was by going in search of my birth family. Archived local newspapers helped me find out I'd got a twin sister abandoned a year after me. Apparently Mum had been ill with cancer when Rebecca was abandoned and couldn't adopt her. Their misplaced guilt had forced them to keep it all secret.

It took me ages but I eventually found my twin. She looks exactly like me with oval face, brown eyes and turned up nose, we're even the same height but *personality wise we couldn't be more different. She's all self-confident and I'm, well, not. She always speaks her mind and does just what she wants.*

Over the summer I went to visit Gran. I missed her so much and it was a good chance to get away from all the tension at home.

Trouble was, as soon as I stepped off the bus, eighteen-year-old creep, Joshua Green tried to chat me up. Then later he cornered me alone. When his hands wandered a lot further than they should I did the only thing a girl could do. I made my knee connect with a part of his body he'd rather it hadn't. With his threats of revenge chasing me like a rabid dog, I made my escape.

The next day Gran was mugged. I like, totally freaked. She wouldn't let me ring my mum because she didn't want her fussing around so I had to deal with everything on my own. Gran lost all her confidence and wouldn't even leave the bungalow. I figured it had to be Joshua and set out to get him arrested so Gran would feel safe again.

I spent most of my holidays trying to do that and Luke and Rebecca even came to help.

If all that wasn't enough Marcy, my birth mum, turned up! Me and Rebecca are like, her doubles from when she was our age. She told me about her husband who made her abandon us and how he beat her so bad she ended up in hospital and him in prison.

I also met my older brother, Mark. He's just like my birth dad, angry and aggressive. Turns out he blames me and Rebecca for just about everything that's wrong in his life. Like, hello, we were just babies!

About a week before I was due home, I heard angry voices in Gran's bungalow. Sneaking in, I found Mark threatening Gran and Rebecca with a knife. I tried to help and there was this massive fight where I nearly got stabbed. But Gran saved me by knocking him out cold! Best of it was, she saved herself as well. Turns out Mark was the one who mugged her and after clonking him on the head she got all her confidence back! The last week of my hols was actually relaxing and fun the way the whole holiday was supposed to be.

But everything has to end and a week before we were due back at school I headed back to Rotherham.

***

CHAPTER ONE

I sank back onto the picnic mat and sighed.

"Now this is the way to spend the hols." I'd just finished telling my friend, Becca about all the trouble I'd faced in Scarborough over the summer.

Becca rolled onto her side to face me, her head resting on the palm of her hand.

"I wish I could've been there for you. It must have been terrifying."

Squinting in the brilliant sunshine I nodded. "It's been like, an absolute nightmare. I mean, I went to Scarborough thinking it'd be a good break from all the conflict around here. Instead I got World War Three."

"Slight exaggeration." Smiling, Becca pushed her glasses higher up her nose then lowered herself back down on the mat.

"Well, yeah." I closed my eyes against the sun, the warm rays making my body feel relaxed and calm. We were lying on a grassy slope, in Clifton Park. Below us kids played on the rides. Their cries and giggles floating up mixed with the rumbling of mini rollercoasters and the occasional squeak of swings. "But it was bad enough. I mean, Joshua touched me up on the first day!" I shuddered. "The sensation of his hands on my waist and under my top, eew, just thinking about it makes me want to throw up."

"Well if that's what you're going to do then face the other way!"

I grinned. Becca had changed so much since plucking up courage to leave evil Emma's gang and join me instead. Being my friend meant instant exclusion. Everybody's too scared that Emma will find out some hidden family secret and announce it to the whole school that they daren't go against her.

The thwack, thwack of a family playing football nearby invaded my ears as my jaw clenched at the thought of her. I wished there was some way to stop Emma and set the whole school free, but I'd no idea how.

"It's no wonder you thought he was the one who mugged your gran; especially after you kneed him in the groin!" Becca paused. "I can't believe it turned out to be your birth brother Mark and that he tried to kill you! Did your life flash before you or anything?"

Before I could answer a shadow crossed my eyes. I opened them and the remaining warmth immediately left my body. Emma stood right in front of me, a knowing smile on her narrow face. She looked so young and innocent with wide green eyes and long black hair tied back in a pony tail. She was anything but.

"Hello, Rachel," she said, her voice sickly sweet.

I sat up, my arms suddenly weak. The holidays were now officially over. Emma was back in my life and that could only mean one thing; trouble.

How long had she been standing there? I was vaguely aware of Becca sitting up beside me as my mind replayed our conversation. Emma's shadow might have just passed my eyes, but she could've been standing behind us for ages. If she wanted new ammunition to use against me, I'd just given it to her.

Forcing myself to speak, I tried to sound relaxed.

"Hello, Emma."

"Nice day, isn't it?" she cooed back.

What was this, friendly chat? We hated each other, why was she doing small talk? Only one answer came to me, because she now had power over me again. She knew things that only Becca, Luke and my family knew. And if I wanted to keep it secret, which I did, she could make me do anything, I'd be her slave. My stomach turned over so fast I had to swallow hard to keep my dinner down.

"Yeah, it's real hot," I said, with a fake smile.

Emma stood slim and straight, her sharp nose and chin raised.

"Well, see you at school next week," she said, her grin wide as she turned and walked away down the grassy slope.

"Do you think she heard?" Becca asked softly, her blue eyes wide behind her glasses. Emma hadn't even acknowledged her.

I nodded. "I don't know how much, but she definitely heard something." I bit my lip. "All I can do now is wait and see how she's gonna use it against me. All I know is that by the time she's finished, my life's gonna be a total misery."

***

CHAPTER TWO

Walking downstairs on the first day of term I felt like a lemming about to jump off a cliff. I just wanted to head back upstairs, bury myself under the covers and stay there, forever.

"Hello, Love. How are you feeling?" Mum sat at the kitchen table, a steaming mug of coffee in her hands. She watched me with eyes full of sympathy. "Are you worried about seeing that Emma girl?

I shrugged.

At the end of last term a tiny few had turned away from Emma for what she'd done to Luke but they hadn't exactly turned towards me instead.

"I made you toast," Mum continued. "Can you manage a couple of slices?"

I shook my head.

"Rachel, I know you're nervous, but you have to eat."

"I'm not hungry, Mum."

"A cuppa, then?"

She stood and walked over to the new wooden cabinets looking slimmer than ever in a tight black T-shirt and black trousers. Why couldn't I have a figure like that? I'd got lumps and bumps everywhere. Sam, my friend in Scarborough, said they were all in the right places but she'd never convince me. One of the downsides of being adopted was having no chance of inheriting any of Mum's slim genes.

"Okay. Yes, please," I said, pulling a chair out from under the table and dropping onto it.

Noticing a small stack of envelopes on the kitchen counter, I asked, "Any word?"

"Not yet," Mum answered, placing a yellow mug in front of me. "But it's only been a month, they can take up to three."

Mum had written a chic lit novel and after receiving several rejections she'd finally lost patience and sent off copies to every publisher in the Writer's and Artist's Year Book. Waiting for replies was absolutely killing her.

"It'll happen, Mum."

Taking a sip of coffee, I clamped my lips together as my stomach heaved.

"I'm going," I managed, picking up my school bag and slinging it over my shoulder. "See you later."

"Bye, Love. I hope it goes okay."

I knew Mum was trying hard to be supportive. Our relationship hadn't been the same since finding out about my adoption. I knew why they'd kept it secret but Mum and Dad had lied to me all my life and that took some getting over.

The kitchen door clicked shut behind me and I walked around the side of the house. As soon as the road came into sight so did Luke. My pace quickened, my body suddenly feeling lighter.

He must have heard my footsteps on the gravel path, because he turned and looked at me, his beautiful blue eyes shining and the breeze playing with his blond hair. With fantastic muscles and a body to die for, not to mention his ability to put up with my drama queen

13

moments, he's the most amazing boyfriend ever. His face split into a gorgeous grin making my whole body feel warm and tingly. I still couldn't believe a great guy like Luke fancied me.

"How're you feeling?" he asked, as I reached him and he slipped his arm around my waist.

A lot better now I've seen you, I thought.

"A bit sick," I said. "I'm just dreading seeing Emma. I know she heard something and won't just let it go. She's gonna want revenge on you for showing her up last term and she hates me. All she's needed is new ammunition and now I've given it to her."

Luke sighed and waited for a double decker bus to roar past before speaking.

"You're right but I wish you weren't. She'll use it somehow, against both of us if she can. It's a pity you've got no other friends at school 'cause you could've just told them yourself and got it over with, like I did."

"Oh, thanks, Luke, make me feel even worse, why don't you?"

"I'm sorry Rach, I'm just saying it like it is. I've been trying to think of an answer for you but I've come up with zip."

I sighed. "I know I should just tell everybody and get it over with, but it's bad enough everybody knowing I'm adopted and my parents lied about it. I don't want them knowing about my crazy birth family as well."

As we got nearer school, more blue and red uniforms joined us and the flipping of my stomach got way faster.

"Hey, you two!" Becca's voice echoed out of the side street we were passing. We stopped to let her catch up. "You ready then?" she asked, tugging her bag higher up her shoulder.

"Nope. You?" I answered.

"Not really," she said, "When am I ever?"

"Hey, Luke!" Liam, one of Luke's friends crossed the road to join us. "You doing footy again?"

"Yep. Kit's in the bag in case there's a practice today," he said, tapping his sports bag with his left hand.

In school term I don't think I've even seen Luke without his sports bag slung over his shoulder. Football, athletics, it didn't matter, he was into it all.

We turned in through the huge iron gates and the school buildings faced us. Built in a horseshoe shape around an open area covered in tarmac they hadn't changed even the green paint was the same.

I heard Becca groan beside me and followed her gaze.

With head high and a grin that oosed confidence, Emma headed towards us. Every eye in the vicinity turned to watch, recognising her purposeful stride that usually meant trouble for somebody. My twisting stomach instantly froze. This was it, she'd waited for the first day of school to get me.

Luke's grip tightened around my waist. Unconsciously we'd all stopped walking and just stood waiting for her poison to spill.

"Hi, Rach!" Emma said when she was close enough.

"Hi." I said, my voice flat.

"I just came to warn you." Her grin spread wider while my jaw set. "There's a new English teacher, they call her Mrs De'Ath. Death, can you believe it? Anyway, Louise says she heard Mrs Death's going to be taking your English group and she's a real

15

hard nut. Louise's mum was the only school governor opposed to her coming. She'd heard of her reputation from a friend who's kid goes to Mrs Death's last school."

"Oh," I said, intelligently. I mean, what was this? When was the attack gonna start?

"Anyway, just thought I'd let you know." Emma grinned, spun around and marched off back to her friends.

"Yeah, thanks." My voice was weak.

"That's okay. What are friends for?" Emma called back before being swallowed up in the sea of blue and red uniforms.

"That was weird," Luke murmured.

"Friends? What's that all about?" Becca asked.

I could only shake my head. Emma was up to something, I just wished I knew what it was.

"You'd better watch out for her," Luke muttered. "Don't trust her."

I nodded, a tight knot in my stomach making me feel even sicker than before. I couldn't get past the feeling that a bomb was about to go off and I'd be somewhere near the epicenter.

***

Mrs De'Ath chewed out just about everybody in English, including one boy just for sneezing. Thankfully, I managed to stay below her radar and escaped without incident.

"How was it?" a voice asked in the corridor afterwards.

I turned to see Emma smiling at me. An antelope finding a lioness grinning at her would probably feel better than I did.

"Er, okay," I said.

"Did you get through it okay?"

16

"Yeah, but Louise got told off for sloppy writing."

Emma grinned. "I keep telling Louise her writing's worse than my doctor's. It's a wonder any teacher can read it."

"Yeah, right," I said. Like what was I supposed to say? This friendly act was seriously freaking me out. But maybe that was her plan?

***

"I don't get it," I told Becca, as we sat on the grass watching Luke kick a football about with his mates. "It's just not normal. What's she up to? It's been two weeks now and she's still being nice."

"Maybe she didn't hear anything," Becca suggested, taking a bite out of her sandwich.

I shrugged. "Maybe. But I think she's planning something. I just wish she'd do whatever it is. Every day my stomach's turning over wondering whether this is the day she'll drop the bomb and my world will explode like it did in April. This friendliness is wearing me down. She even congratulated me when I scored at netball yesterday."

"Maybe she's changed. You know, she saw how everybody sided with Luke when she tried to bad mouth him. It might've made her think. I haven't noticed her being horrible to anybody this term. She's even made friends with Carly Thompson!"

I chewed my ham sandwich, thinking back over the last two weeks. Maybe Becca was right. I mean, Carly Thompson was a bully, she even threatened me on my first day at Riverside Comp. Emma and Carly hated each other, or at least they used to. I shook my head.

"I still can't believe it. Emma turning into a nice person? Can a boiled sweet turn into icecream?"

17

No matter how long we talked I still didn't have any answers. All I knew was that the feeling of unease in my mind just kept on growing.

***

CHAPTER THREE

Another two weeks passed and others noticed the change in Emma as well. Girls who'd ignored me since April began talking to me again. I even got invited to a couple of parties. It'd been a month and I actually started to believe that everything was gonna be okay.

The good things didn't end there. When I got home the first Monday in October, Mum bounced to the door, a white envelope clutched in her hands.

"It's a yes! Rachel, it's a yes! I'm going to be published!"

"What? No!" Grabbing the envelope from her, I pulled out the letter and read it, my eyes widening with every word. "Mum, that's great!" I could feel the huge grin on my face.

"At last," she said, bouncing up and down like a kid on Christmas morning.

"So what happens now?" Warm sparks shot around my body, catching my mum's excitement.

"They're drawing up a contract and they want to meet me. They said they'll be in touch."

Flinging my arms around her, I squeezed hard. Mum's arms wrapped around me, her hug so tight, I could barely breathe.

For the first time in months I actually felt really happy.

***

When I arrived home from school two days later a red-headed stranger smiled at me. She stood beside the open double glass doors to our lounge holding an expensive looking camera.

"Is this your daughter?" she asked, looking young and casual with a pony tail, baggy jumper and tight jeans.

"Yes," Mum said, "Rachel, this is Mandy Sherman, she's a photographer from the Times. They're doing an article about my book being signed."

"Great, Mum!" Wow, this was really coming together for her. "I'll head upstairs and let you get on with it."

"Actually," Mandy spoke before Mum had a chance. "A picture of the two of you would be good. A mother and daughter feel to the article?"

Mum looked at me, her eyebrows raised. I shrugged. I never minded having my picture taken but definitely not in this uniform.

"Has she time to change?" Mum asked, reading my expression.

Mandy glanced at her watch.

"Five minutes?"

Grinning, I nodded. I could do five minutes.

A quick change and several photos later, Mum saw Mandy out then joined me in the lounge.

I dropped onto our beige leather settee and watched Mum settle into her matching chair under the window, a satisfied smile, playing on her lips.

"When's the article going to be in?" I asked.

"She couldn't say," Mum answered. "Within the next couple of weeks, she thinks."

"Fame, at last, eh, Mum?" I grinned.

Mum grinned back. We were slowly beginning to feel like family again.

***

"Are you okay?"

It was the Thursday before October half term and I huddled close to Luke in the cold wind. Cars whizzed past as we walked along Clifton Lane then into the sheltered gardens of Clifton Park.

"What?" He looked dazed like I'd just woken him from a dream.

"Are you okay?" I asked again as we settled onto a bench overlooking the flowerless rockeries, "You haven't said a word since we left school."

"Yeah, I'm fine," he murmured.

"All right what was I talking about, then?" My hands slipped onto my hips, a mannerism I'd caught off Rebecca.

Luke frowned, "You were talking about … about a newspaper."

He definitely didn't sound sure.

"I was telling you that the picture of me and mum is in the paper today! My claim to fame and you're not even listening!"

"I'm sorry, Rach." He ran his hand through his beautiful blond hair. A move that made my knees weak and my heart flutter like a trapped butterfly.

"Luke?"

"Yeah?"

"You know how you always say you can read my expressions?"

"Yeah."

"Well right now, I can read yours. Running your hands through your hair coupled with that little frown, means you're worried. So what is it? Is it Matt? Has something happened to him in prison?"

"No! No, Matt's fine." Luke sighed. "It's us."

Shutters flipped down over my heart, turning everything black.

"You don't want to go out with me anymore." I'd always known it couldn't last, I mean, he's so fit, why would he want me? I'm just plain, with enough problems to drive anybody away.

"No! It's not that!" Luke's eyes were wide. "It's just the opposite." He sighed again, his jaw working. "It's Emma. Well, Carly actually."

The shutters, having lifted at his denial, dropped right back down again and latched shut.

"Okay, what's going on?" My voice was flat, resigned. I knew this friendly attitude of Emma's was too good to last.

Luke turned to face me.

"Emma must have heard you, Rach. I don't know how much she knows, but it's enough. It looks like her friendship and getting everyone being okay with you was just so it'll be worse if everything goes back the way it was. Carly confronted me today and said that Emma still really fancies me. She said she's made you happy and deserves something in return. Me. Carly said I should leave you and go out with Emma or you might find your family secrets leaking out. Then everybody would …," he paused. "This is her words, not mine. Everybody would think you're psycho like the rest of your birth family."

I'd been expecting this since the summer but I still couldn't stop tears pricking my eyes.

"After all that's happened, she still wants you to be her boyfriend?"

Luke nodded. "Seems like it. Carly's making out it's all her idea as a friend of Emma's but I'm not buying that. Emma's got to be pulling the strings. I think it's more a power thing now. I've shown her up for what she really is. There's people who aren't in her pocket anymore. I think if I'm her boyfriend it'll show everybody she can still make anybody do what she wants, even if it takes some time. Then they'll be scared of her again."

Shaking my head, I knew he was right. This was Emma and her deceitful scheming through and through. It took a matter of seconds for me to know what to do.

"Tell her no," I said, my voice way more determined than I felt.

"But she'll tell everybody." Luke's face was filled with concern for me, his hands tight on my shoulders.

"I know, but we're not playing Emma's stupid game anymore." My teeth ground together. "I'll take my chances."

***

All was quiet the next day at school but I couldn't rest. I knew Luke was gonna find Carly at break and tell her he wasn't playing along with her scheming. I spent the second half of the morning watching everybody, wondering when the stares and whispering would begin.

"So, did you tell her?" I asked him at lunch. It was raining so we'd opted to meet in the dining hall. We'd chosen a table way back in the furthest corner away from everybody, so we could talk without being overheard. With the racket of laughter, chatting and clattering cutlery we stood a great chance of keeping our conversation private.

23

"Yeah," he said. "I couldn't find her earlier but caught up with her just before meeting you.

"No wonder it's been quiet then. I've been expecting explosions ever since break." The end of my thumb crept into my mouth and I chewed the nail, a habit I'd picked up from Becca.

"Well, don't look now, but Carly and Emma's heads are so close at the table over there they could be swapping nits."

I turned and looked over the sea of heads to Emma's usual table in the centre of the room. One black and one blonde head were meshed so close together they were almost one.

"Great. Well, I've had five peaceful weeks I suppose I should be happy, it's the longest I've had at this school without trouble."

As we kissed and went to our different afternoon classes I felt like a kitten separated from its mum. With every whisper or glance I shrank further into myself, believing every conversation was about me. I longed for the bell to ring so I could escape. Trouble was, after half term, I'd have to come back.

***

CHAPTER FOUR

I didn't eat or sleep much that week. I spent most of my time with Luke, trying not to think about going back to school. Rebecca was on holiday in Cos but promised to come round the following Monday. Becca was busy with her family. We talked on the phone, but her voice sounded flat. I guess she was wishing she'd never become friends with a loser like me. Sam was real sympathetic but couldn't really do anything except listen. She at least cheered me up a bit by telling me the twinkle was well and truly back in Gran's eyes. She was going to the day centre again and out shopping without any fear at all. She was even cheating at Scrabble! After worrying about her all summer that was one bit of good news I was glad to hear.

***

By the time Monday finally rolled around I had dark circles under my eyes, a pounding head and spent the morning in the bathroom retching. Mum was all like, 'are you all right, Rachel? Have you got a bug? Do you need to stay home?' Now that was *sooo* tempting. But leaving it a few days would be worse because they'd know I was scared and hiding out.

"No, I'm all right, Mum," I said, standing up straight and holding my stomach when it threatened to retch again. I'd been in there so long it felt like I'd been through a boxing match and lost. "Must be something I ate. But I'm all right now," I lied.

I knew I should've told Mum about it but she'd have insisted on seeing Mrs Pendlebury. Next it'd be, either, 'tough it out, Rachel, it'll pass'; or 'would you like to change schools?' And I didn't want to hear it. I just wanted to get through the first day and see how bad it was gonna be.

Luke was waiting outside for me and I ran into his arms. Feeling them wrapped around me, I instantly felt safer.

"That bad, is it?" He breathed into my hair.

I nodded. "I've been throwing up all morning." Then cringed, I mean, not exactly romantic talk when my boyfriend's arms were enfolding me. "Well, I, er, would have if I'd eaten anything, you know?"

Luke grinned lopsidedly, "Yeah, I know what you mean."

As we approached school my stomach cramped so tight it felt like I'd done fifty situps. Clamping my mouth shut, I tried to swallow back the sick feeling.

"You okay?" Luke looked down at me as we walked closer.

"Hm hm," I nodded, not daring to speak.

"Only, my ribs and hand think you're way tense."

I looked up questioning, then realised my grip on him had tightened so much my fingers were actually aching.

"Sorry." My cheeks burned as I released my grip.

"It's okay, look don't let them get to you, all right?"

"Okay."

As we walked through the gate heads turned in our direction. Some smirked, others just stared then turned back to their groups, whispering and casting furtive glances in my direction.

"It begins," Luke murmured, "Sorry, Rach."

"It's not your fault," I told him. "It's my defective birth family."

"Yeah, but it's me she fancies. If I was ugly we'd be okay."

"If you were ugly I wouldn't want you either," I managed, trying to stay cheerful despite the stares.

"Oh, and I thought you loved my personality," Luke joked.

"That's part of it, but definitely not all." I looked up at him and smiled but it disappeared quickly when he kissed me and headed off to his form room.

As I walked into registration, all heads turned. Emma had her back to me but knew I was there.

"I feel so sorry for her. I mean, what must it be like having a demented brother try to murder you?"

"And a father who wanted you dead at birth," Leah, one of my ex-friends added. Since I'd left Emma's 'inner circle' Leah had been promoted from the fringes.

"And a mother who dumps you," chirped up tiny, blonde Jessica, another promotee, taking Becca's place.

"It's a wonder she's not crazy herself," Leah added, flicking her long black hair over her shoulders.

"Well, how can you be sure she isn't? Oh, Rachel, you're there," Emma said, all wide-eyed and innocent, "I didn't see you come in."

"Yeah, sure," I said, using every ounce of willpower to slip into my seat rather than launch myself at her and claw her lying face to shreds.

"So sorry to hear about your ..." she paused for effect. "Unfortunate birth family. It must be terrible to find you come from such ... warped stock." Giggles fluttered around the room like butterflies. "It really is shameless the way someone has spread these unsavory truths about your family. It must be so embarrassing."

Her look of fake sympathy made staying in my chair really hard.

"I guess if you knew who it was, you'd want to beat the crap out of them," Jessica said, her nose tilted up in her usual superior way.

"You'd have to watch that though. I mean, it might set something off in you," Leah added. "You could have psychotic tendencies like the rest of your birth family."

"Oh, Leah!" Emma looked shocked, "You can't really mean that? I mean, if that were true then none of us would be safe."

My hands tightened on my desk.

"Well she did attack you last term," Leah said with a worried frown, so fake she'd make a Barbie doll look real.

"She attacked Carly as well," Mandy, another girl in class, piped up, her eyes narrowed at me.

"Mrs Pendlebury should really do something about this," her friend Abbey added, "Anything could happen.

"Don't be stupid," Jodie sneered, ginger hair hanging low over her eyes, "Just 'cause her birth family's weird doesn't mean she is."

Gratitude surged through me like a warm tide.

"Well you're a slapper just like the rest of your family," Leah spat. "What's your mother on now? Her fifth kid with erm, let me see," she put her finger to her lips, "Her fifth man? Your sister's out of school 'cause

28

she got knocked up and you had an abortion last year. Seems you're just like your birth family."

Jodie's face turned scarlet. "Just shut your face, Leah!" she snapped.

Silence filled the room, everybody staring at Jodie, including me. I'd no idea about the abortion and by the look on most other faces neither had anybody else. Another Emma fact, I suppose.

My chest hurt, I wanted to make it all go away, turn back time and stop Jodie speaking up for me so her secret would still be safe, but I couldn't.

Faint muttering started and slowly spread around the room, about both of us. Accusing and worried eyes flicked in both our directions. Emma quietly smirked before turning her back to me, her job done. The urge to hit her was so strong I could barely stay in my seat. Every part of me burned but I couldn't do anything, if I did it'd only convince them they were right.

I'd been tried, convicted and sentenced without even getting chance to say a word, but then that's what everybody likes, juicy gossip.

"I'm sorry," I told Jodie, as we left the room ten minutes later.

"Just leave me alone!" she hissed before marching away.

I watched her go. Great, she'd fallen out with me before we'd even made friends.

By lunch time the rumours had mutated and grown. Mark was a convicted murderer, birth dad was in prison for beating Marcy almost to death and torturing me and Rebecca. I was seeing a psychiatrist for attacking somebody at my old school and my adoptive family had kept it a secret so that Riverside would accept me.

When I walked down the corridor at lunch, everybody dodged out of my way, shying back like I was wielding an axe or something. The whispering had become really quiet like they were scared I'd flip out and kill them if they upset me.

"There's one good thing," I said, as I walked to the sports field with Becca. "Nobody's calling names or hitting me this time, I think they're too scared." I tried to laugh but it came out all broken and shaky. Truth was, this was killing me. I'd only just got used to people being nice to me and now I felt like a criminal. I was being ostracised because of my birth family and a load of rumours. The whispering behind hands while looking in my direction was just as bad as having somebody come and plant a fist in my face. Maybe worse.

An aching void filled my chest and I rambled on, trying to ignore it until I realised Becca wasn't speaking. Stopping, I turned to her.

"What's the matter, Becca? You're not nervous being around me as well are you? You don't believe any of this?"

"No!" Becca's response was quick, her eyes wide but when she didn't say any more I wasn't exactly reassured.

"So, what's the matter? Are you fed up of being associated with the school outcast?" I tried to read her expression. "You don't want to go back to Emma, do you?"

I held my breath, knowing I couldn't take it if Becca turned against me as well. Since leaving Emma's gang she'd been my only real friend at school, other than Luke.

Becca sighed and turned her head away, looking out over the fields.

"You're the best friend I've ever had," she said softly, "I know it's not been easy, but you're the only person who's ever accepted me for who I am. Most people make fun of me for being shy and fat, or use me, like Emma, because Mum and Dad have loads of money. But you've never asked me for anything except friendship and I don't want to lose it."

"Well you won't," I said, trying to figure out where all this was going, "I'm not going to stop being your friend."

Becca turned back to me. "Rachel, Dad's got a new job."

"That's great!" The apologetic look on Becca's face told me there was more. "Isn't it?"

"Rach, it's in London."

That was it. A truck hit me in the chest and I couldn't breathe. Becca was moving to London, same country but far enough away to be gone for good. London was at least four hours drive. Sam in Scarborough was only two hours away and I only ever saw her in the holidays. I'd never see Becca and she definitely wouldn't be here at school with me.

My legs wouldn't support me anymore and I flopped down onto the grass.

"When?" was all I could manage.

"This weekend."

"What?" My head shot up. I stared at her unbelieving. "What about selling your house, arranging the move, working his notice?"

"It's the same company," Becca said, tears in her eyes. "He's got a promotion. He knew it was possible a month ago but didn't want to say anything in case it didn't happen. It's been confirmed now. We've already got a house in London, we used to live down there about five years ago. There's been lodgers living

31

in it but Dad gave them a month's notice as soon as he heard about the possible promotion. They've already moved out and it's all ready for us to move in. Mum's got cleaners in to tidy the place up before we get there. Dad's keeping this house on in case he wants to come up some time for any branch meetings. So there's really not much for us to do. We spent half term packing, that's why I couldn't come round." She hung her head. "I was putting off telling you."

I just sat there shaking my head. Could anything get any worse? I'd only have Luke now and he wasn't in any of my classes. I mean, he might be a brilliant boyfriend but a girlfriend permanently limpetted to his side would soon get on his nerves. A boy needs time with his mates. Mates, something I hadn't got. Come Monday I'd be down to zero in that category.

"I'm sorry, Rach. I really am," Becca said, lowering herself down onto the grass beside me. "I've told Dad I don't want to go but it makes no difference, he's really up on the dad being the head of the household thing."

"Doesn't he even listen to your mum?"

"Sometimes, but Mum agrees with him on this." Becca shrugged. "She likes to buy nice things. The more Dad earns the more she can spend; clothes, furniture and stuff. Sometimes I think 'things' are more important to her than anything else, including me."

Becca plucked at the grass, her chin almost on her knees.

"Oh, Becca, I'm sorry." I reached out and touched her arm. "Here I am thinking about how this'll affect me and I haven't even thought about how you must be feeling. Great friend I am."

"You're the best friend I've ever had!" Becca said, taking off her glasses and wiping her eyes. "I'm going to miss you *so* much!"

I couldn't stop my own tears escaping as I reached out and hugged her.

"I'll miss you too!"

Neither of us noticed Luke approaching.

"Are you okay?" he asked, crouching down in front of us. "I've heard all the rumours. Has it got too bad?"

I shook my head, looking at him through misty eyes, "No. Well yes, but it's not that, it's Becca, she's leaving."

"Leaving?" Luke's eyes widened. "Leaving for where?"

"London," Becca said with a sniff. "Dad's got a new job. We're going this weekend."

"Woa! This weekend?" Luke stared at Becca then me. "What're you going to do, Rach?"

"I don't know," I whispered. "I suppose, I'll just have to get on with it." Heaviness spread all through my body like weights hanging from every organ and limb.

"We've still got a week."

That was just like Becca, trying to squeeze a minute positive out of a rotten situation.

I couldn't face my sandwiches as we sat and watched Luke play. He'd already thrown his lunch down his throat in about ten seconds flat so he'd have plenty of time to kick a football around with his mates. Becca, unhappy though she was, still managed to polish off her lunch and most of mine as well.

She wasn't in any of my classes that afternoon and I got a real taste of what everyday was gonna be like when she left. Nobody spoke, choosing to stare and whisper instead until the teacher told them to pack it in.

***

"Becs this is impossible!" I moaned to my twin that evening. I hadn't eaten any of my tea and got a lecture from Mum, although she toned it down when I told her about Becca leaving. Instead she just walked about with this worried frown, muttering to herself about weight loss and anorexia.

Rebecca sat in Mum's chair under the window in the lounge, her jean clad legs drawn up beneath her.

"Well, there is one answer," she said after thinking for like, five minutes.

"What's that?" I asked, without much hope. Knowing Rebecca's sense of humour she'd probably suggest throwing myself under a bus or something then it'd all be over.

"You could move to my school."

I gawped, totally speechless.

"Don't look so shocked, people move schools all the time when they're bullied and that. And, let's face it, you're hardly happy at Riverside Comp, are you?"

"But what about Luke?" I couldn't imagine being away from him.

"Well, he'd still exist. He could move as well if he wanted or you could still see him on evenings."

I stared down at the carpet. "I don't know, I've never thought of anything like that. I'd really miss seeing Luke at break and lunch… but he'd have some time away from me. It'd probably do him good, I mean, nobody wants a clingy girlfriend."

"Give over!" Rebecca scoffed. "A beautiful girl like you! He'd be crazy not to want you around."

"I'm not beautiful!"

34

"Hey! You're my identical twin and I'm beautiful so you must be as well. The only difference is the length of our hair, my short bob definitely looks better."

"Yeah, sure," I said, "And don't forget my extra twenty pounds in weight."

"Twenty pounds, yeah, right, more like six." Rebecca shook her head. "Look, I've gotta go now or I'll miss my bus. Just think about it, okay?"

"Okay."

I stood and walked her to the door. As she stepped out, she turned back and gave me a hug.

"It'll all work out, you'll see," she said.

I wished I shared her confidence. Watching her walk down the road and disappear out of sight with a last wave, I couldn't help wondering how twins could be so different. Closing the door I turned back to the lounge to think it all through. Changing schools was like, huge. It'd mean traveling an hour a day, hardly ever seeing Luke, probably not even being in the same classes as Rebecca. It'd mean starting all over again and what if they didn't like me? I could cut my hair short so they'd think I was Rebecca, but what then? Did I really want to pretend to be my twin sister just so I'd have friends? I mean, I was popular back in Scarborough, I had a great bunch of friends there and got on with everybody. Why was I having such a hard time in Rotherham? The answer shot straight into my head, Emma. At Riverside Comp if Emma's against you, you might as well pack up and go because that was it, social leper forever.

I thought about it all evening and most of the night as well. By the next morning my head was pounding. I managed three bites of toast then had to stop, any more and I'd have thrown up. Mum watched me with a worried frown but managed not to say anything. She wouldn't last much longer. A 'let's sit down and have a talk', session was coming very soon. At least there was one plus, the extra twenty pounds wouldn't be there much longer if I kept eating like a hamster. In fact there'd not be much of me left at all.

***

At school the whisperings continued, even the year sevens were looking at me like I was a raving lunatic about to pounce. One boy dodged out of my way so fast he fell into a bucket the caretaker was using to clean the hallway windows. It would've been funny if it wasn't so pathetic.

Walking between French and Maths I felt a sharp jab in my ribs.

"Flipped out lately, Brooks?" Carly sneered, looming over me like a blonde gorilla. "Go on, let's see it. All your family's violent nut jobs, let's see you flip out. Then you can wear one of those lovely white jackets, you know, the ones that fasten at the back. Bet they've got a whole selection just for your family."

Clenching my jaw tight I fought to keep my hands at my sides and my mouth shut. She wanted me to respond to prove her right. I wasn't gonna give her the satisfaction. I just kept on walking.

"Go on then, run away! Coward!" Her voice followed me down the corridor making everybody I passed turn and stare.

With stinging eyes I reached Maths and sank into my chair, keeping my head down. I couldn't win. If I hit her I was psycho and Emma was proved right, if I ignored her I was a coward. I just wanted the day to end.

As soon as lunch came I headed straight outside, found Becca and Luke and stayed with them.

We sat on the grass with our jackets tight against the cold.

"Aren't you playing today?" I asked Luke, as his friends chased a football in front of us.

Luke shrugged, "Not in the mood."

"Why?"

"Just not."

"Is this because of me?" I twisted to look at him, but he just gazed straight ahead.

"It's nothing, okay?"

Taking my arm from around his waist I looked out over the field. After the morning I'd had so far, the last thing I needed was Luke having a moody. If he didn't want to talk then I was probably the reason. Maybe he was wishing he'd never become my boyfriend. I mean, after the bullying at his old school he really wanted to be popular but going out with the school outcast wasn't exactly helping.

Becca was no better, she just gazed at the horizon as well, lost in her own thoughts.

After that uplifting lunch I headed off to biology with Becca. I'd looked forward to having her in a class with me but her silence wasn't exactly promising.

As we crossed the tarmac she took my arm and pulled me to one side away from the stream of bodies heading in.

"Rach, I've got to tell you something," she said.

"Why? What's up?" My heart started pounding just at the tone of her voice.

"I was coming out of Spanish first period this morning when I saw Louise and Luke in the corridor."

A lump formed in my throat.

"I figured something was up so I crept out and hid just around the corner from them. I know I shouldn't have been spying but I was worried about Luke and you."

"Go on."

Becca shook her head. "You're not gonna like it," she whispered.

***

CHAPTER FIVE

"I'll try and tell you what she said but I can't get it exactly word for word, okay?"

"Okay," I agreed.

"Well, Louise kept her voice low but I was close enough to hear," Becca continued. "She stood real close to Luke and asked how you were coping. He said, 'Like you care.' She said, 'I do. I just don't want it to get worse for her. I mean, she was my friend.' He asked what she was trying to say. She said that no matter how unhappy you were now, things could get a whole lot worse and she didn't want that to happen."

I inwardly shuddered. What was going on now?

"Luke asked what webs they were spinning," Becca said, "And Louise was all like, 'Who says we're spinning any webs? I'd just recommend you consider a relationship with Emma, it'd be in Rachel's best interests.'"

"What did he say to that?" My voice came out as a whisper. There was no air in my lungs for anything more.

"He didn't, she just went on and said, 'Something could happen that'd make Rachel more miserable than she's ever been.' I peeked round and saw her running a finger down his chest as she said,

'You wouldn't want that for Rachel, would you? There's some things people would never recover from. Think about it, and who knows, if you make the right decision everything could get better for Rachel, people might even start talking to her again.'" Becca watched me with large sad eyes. I just wanted to drop onto the floor, curl up in a ball and disappear forever.

"What do you think it is, Becca?" I asked, "What else has Emma got on me?"

I couldn't think. She'd already devastated me back in April with the news of my abandonment and adoption. Now she'd told the whole school about my violent birth family, what else was there? One thing I did know was that Emma and co didn't make idle threats. Whatever it was, I wasn't going to like it one little bit. I just wished she'd told Luke what it was then it'd be easier to decide what to do.

"What did Luke tell her?"

"He slapped her hand away then told her they were evil, conniving witches and he hated the sight of them."

I smiled at that one.

"Did he tell her to get lost?"

Becca didn't answer.

"Becca?"

She shook her head. "Louise said he could say what he liked but Emma wanted him as her pet and she always gets what she wants, no matter what the cost. And did he really want you to pay the price?"

"What did he say?"

"He didn't, he just turned and walked away. I guess that's why he was so quiet at lunch."

"I've got to talk to him!" I looked around as though expecting him to still be sitting on the grass waiting for me to come back.

"You can't, he'll be in his next class by now."

I growled with frustration. "Why didn't you tell me earlier Becca? I could've talked it out with him. Now I've got to wait until after school and he might have done something stupid by then. You know what he's like for protecting me."

"I'm sorry, Rach, but there was no chance. Luke was already with me when you came out to lunch."

I sighed, "It's okay, Becca. I just wish you'd said you felt sick or something so I could've gone to the toilets with you. Then you could've told me."

"I'm sorry, I didn't think." Becca looked close to tears. What was I doing to her? Knowing me was ruining hers and Luke's lives. Suddenly I knew what I had to do. Becca would be gone by the end of the week, she'd be okay but I had to save Luke. If I wasn't there Emma would have no more ammunition. I'd tell him after school, I was gonna change schools. I was gonna go to Swinton with Rebecca.

***

Walking along the street towards my house with cars whizzing past, Luke stopped, took hold of my shoulders and fixed me with his gaze. "You can't do that! You can't let Emma chase you out of school!"

I sighed. "Luke, neither of us will have any peace while ever I'm there and you know it. Emma's got her heart set on owning you and she won't stop until she succeeds."

"That won't change when you're gone."

"No, but she won't be able to use me to get to you. She's already used everything she knows about you and it hasn't got her anywhere. Me and my dysfunctional birth family are a gift to her. She'll use every tiny little detail she can to pressure you and attack

41

me. My life'll be a misery while ever I'm there and so will yours."

Even through my determination, I could feel the tears prick my eyes. I didn't want to be away from Luke. I couldn't bear the thought of being at another school and not seeing him at breaks and lunch.

Luke's shoulders sagged, his head slowly shaking.

"I hate to let her win but, if it's what you really want Rach, then it's okay with me. It's just that we'll never see each other what with homework and my football practice."

All I could do was nod, my bottom lip trembling so much I knew I'd start to bawl if I said anything.

Luke's arms wrapped around my shoulders and drew me in. With my face pressed against his warm chest, hearing his heart beat through the thin cotton, the tears came. I knew his shirt was getting soaked but Luke didn't say anything, he just held me there until my sobs slowed and my breathing calmed.

"Rach, you know, whether you're at our school or Swinton, I'll always be there for you. You know that, don't you?"

I nodded, feeling like I'd just lost a boyfriend.

Luke was so handsome and fit, he was bound to find somebody else, somebody who didn't carry all this emotional baggage. I left him on the pavement and walked up our drive wishing there was an alternative, but knowing there wasn't. I had to move for Luke's sake so he could be free of Emma once and for all.

Once inside I went straight up to my room and texted Rebecca to ring me asap. Then I flopped down on my bed feeling totally empty. I was losing everything, Luke, Becca, I'd already lost my home in

Scarborough, all my old friends and my gran. Everybody I knew eventually faded away, only my mum and dad were consistent. I wondered how long it would take for them to turn from me or for me to have to leave them. They were already one step further away now I knew they weren't my birth parents. Soon I'd have nothing and nobody left.

I picked up my mobile and rang Gran.

"Hey, Gran, how're you doing?" I asked, trying to sound cheerful.

"I'm fine, fit as a fiddle now and how's my favourite granddaughter?"

"I'm your only granddaughter."

"Picky, picky," Gran said. "Well, I must say, you're doing well. A couple of phone calls every week since the holidays. I must have really worried you this summer."

"Just keeping my promise," I said, smiling. "I've been texting Sam as well."

"Are you all right, Love?"

I shook my head. Gran knew me better than anybody, she could always pick up on my moods.

"I'm fine," I lied, "It's just been a tiring day."

"You would tell me if anything's bothering you; wouldn't you?"

Great, now I'd got Gran worried.

"Yeah, course I would. I'm fine, I've just got a pile of maths homework and I'm not looking forward to it." Now that wasn't a lie.

"Okay, Sweetheart. I'll let you get back to it then. Don't want to use all your phone credit on me. You might need to phone your friends for help with those complicated maths questions."

If I had any friends.

"Okay, Gran, ring you again soon."

"Bye, Sweetheart."

"Bye, Gran."

I ended the call and slowly put the mobile down. I really missed her.

An hour later when Rebecca still hadn't rung, I texted her again. I didn't dare ring incase her dad was there. He still didn't know we were in touch and he'd burst a blood vessel if he thought she and her mum had gone behind his back. Put it this way, their tentative beginnings of reunion would explode in a burst of volcanic anger.

***

The next morning Rebecca still hadn't rung, she hadn't texted either.

"Maybe she's changed her mind," I told Luke as we walked to school. "Maybe she's decided having a double at school isn't exactly the best idea after all and she just can't face telling me."

"Rebecca, can't face telling you? Yeah, sure, she'd tell a lion its breath stank just before it bit her head off! She might just be out of credit," Luke said, obviously trying to calm me before I built myself up into a self-pitying frenzy.

"Yeah, maybe," I said, unconvinced.

"Why don't you ring her now? She'll be away from her dad but not in any classes yet."

He'd got a point. I could at least ask whether she'd changed her mind. I pulled out my mobile and speed dialed her.

"Hi, this is Becs leave a message after the beep and if I like you I'll ring you back."

I smiled, that was Rebecca all right.

"Hey, Becs, give me a ring, okay? I've been thinking about your school and might want to change, but it's okay if you've changed your mind. Look, ring me, okay?"

"Not answering?" Luke asked, eyebrows raised.

I shook my head. "Might be going into school," I said, trying to convince myself more than Luke, "Or maybe it's on silent and she didn't hear it."

"Yeah, that could be it." Now Luke didn't sound so convinced. "So, what do you want me to do about Emma?"

We were still a couple of streets from school and I slowed right down. I wanted him to tell her to get lost, but I'd wanted to be sure I could move away before he said anything.

My mind scanned for possibilities, but inside I already knew the answer. Whatever Emma had planned for me she'd just have to do it because there was no way I'd let Luke be her slave again. I mean, what was up with her anyway? Wouldn't she rather have a boyfriend who actually loved her? But then, everybody knew what she was like, maybe no boy wanted the hassle of trying to please her all the time.

"Tell her to get lost," I said, feeling like my words should've been accompanied by a drum roll or a thunderclap or something. "She'll just have to do her worst."

Why did my stomach just feel like I'd been issued with the death penalty? Somebody had their hands inside me and was kneading it like dough.

"You sure?" Luke's arm tightened around my shoulders as the school came into sight.

"Hm, hmn," I nodded not daring to speak.

"Okay, but I'll avoid her gang if I can to give you more time to talk to Rebecca."

Once inside the school gates, Luke lowered his head and we shared a lingering kiss, not caring who saw us. That actually strengthened my resolve, those lips were mine and there was no way Emma was getting anywhere near them, not ever again.

I just wished I knew what she was planning. What else had she found out to hurt me? Maybe I'd got a birth great-grandparent who was hung for murder or something? I smiled at that one, if Emma didn't ease up I'd be tempted to follow in their footsteps. One thing was certain, Emma would stop nowhere in her search for dirt. Just a pity she wasn't as thorough in her efforts to find true friends rather than people who were just too frightened to be her enemies.

***

"I ran into Louise," Luke said, as we sat in our usual spot staring out over the school fields. Becca was using her lunch break to finish an art project she hoped would merit a place on the wall, sort of a memento of her time at Riverside.

"Oh." I rubbed the ribbed strap on my school bag.

"Sorry, I couldn't avoid her. Emma was at one end of the corridor so I went the other way and ran into Louise, instead."

"What happened?"

"She asked if I'd made my decision."

"And?"

Luke plucked a blade of grass and twirled it in his fingers.

"I told her to tell Emma, 'No'"

"What did she say?"

"She just smirked and said, 'so be it, you obviously don't love Rachel as much as everybody thinks.'"

He looked at me, his eyes boring into mine.

"But I do Rach. I love you enough to do anything for you." He paused, looked down, then back up again. "Anything."

Snuggling closer to him, I took his hand in mine. "I know Luke, but I could never let you do that. And anyway, seeing you with Emma would be way worse than anything she could do to me."

"Are you sure?" His thumb stroked the back of my hand.

"Yeah, I'm sure," I said, wishing I really was. "So, I suppose now I wait."

"I don't think you'll have to wait long."

"No, neither do I."

***

I tried Rebecca's mobile again before going back into school but still no answer.

All afternoon I waited for Emma's bombshell, but it never came and I walked out at 3.15 totally bemused. She had to have her weapon ready otherwise she wouldn't have chosen now to threaten us, so why hadn't she used it? Maybe she was making me wait to torture me more and it was working. I just wanted to find out what she had on me then I could start dealing with it. Not knowing and being constantly on edge was way worse. I think.

I rang Rebecca on the way home and her voicemail chirped the same message.

"Where do you think she is?" I asked Luke as we stood at the bottom of our drive, his hands on my hips and his body pressed wonderfully against me.

He shrugged, his head coming down and his lips meeting mine. Wrapping my arms around his neck and losing myself in his kiss, all thoughts of Rebecca vanished. Right now there was nobody else in the world except Luke and me. I couldn't even hear the cars on the road behind him or the footsteps of passing pedestrians.

"You want to come in for a bit?" I asked when we surfaced for air.

"Okay, I'll just text Mum."

Luke tapped away at his phone as we crunched up our drive and in the front door.

"Mum, I'm going up to my room with Luke, we're gonna do homework!" I called.

"Well, just make sure homework is all you're doing!" her muffled voice called back from the kitchen. "I'll be checking!"

I rolled my eyes, shaking my head. Luke just grinned, although his cheeks were a bit on the pink side.

"Is Luke staying for tea?"

I looked up at him and he nodded.

"Yeah, Mum. What're we having?"

"Chips and stew."

I licked my lips, Mum's stew was totally delicious.

***

At six we all sat in the lounge, trays on our laps and plates piled with chips covered in delicious stew.

Dad reached for the remote and switched to the Calendar news bulletin. I stabbed a chip and looked up at the TV just in time to see a large image of my face staring back at me. The fork and chip hovered in front of my mouth as the newsreader announced.

"Fifteen-year-old, Rebecca Chambers was last seen leaving her house in Swinton, South Yorkshire shortly after school on Monday last, reportedly to visit a friend. However, none of her friends saw her that evening and the outgoing teenager hasn't been seen since. Police are asking for anyone with any information about Rebecca's whereabouts to ring this number."

A number appeared beneath Rebecca's chin as my mouth hung wide and an icy hand squeezed my heart. Rebecca was with me Monday night and she never made it home. I could still see her waving as she walked down our drive and along our street. Something happened to her shortly after that.

Rebecca was missing.

My twin was gone.

***

CHAPTER SIX

"Rebecca," I gasped. Already tears were running down my cheeks, I wasn't even sure when I'd started crying.

"Oh, Rachel, Love." Mum's tray was on the floor and she was kneeling beside me, her arms wrapped around my shoulders.

"That poor girl," Dad's voice was soft, reverent.

"She was here," I whispered. "She was here Monday."

My breathing was real shallow, my heart slow like I was drowning. This couldn't be real, Rebecca couldn't be gone.

I looked up at Luke sitting beside me, his eyes wide and face white.

"She was here," I said again.

"Here, Love, drink your tea. It's got sugar in it." Mum thrust the cup into my hands. I looked down at the brown liquid slopping around. Until then I hadn't realised my hands were shaking so badly. "Here, let me hold it," she said, taking the cup back. She held it up to my lips and I drank, like a child. I was too stunned to argue.

"We should ring the police." Dad's voice was flat.

"Why?" Mum's head spun around, her hands tilting and almost spilling the tea down me.

"She was here, Janet." Dad's voice was impatient, like he was speaking to a three-year-old. "The police don't know where she went after she left her house, but we do."

"She's not supposed to come here," I said, my mind still filled with a kind of mist.

"I know, Love, but the police will be looking around Swinton for her, when they actually need to start here," Dad said, slowly, like I was thick or something. But that's how I felt, befuddled, like I wasn't really there and could only watch everything unfold.

"Her mum and dad will fight," I murmured.

"Darling, I think their disagreements are the last thing on their minds right now. We have to think about Rebecca." Dad stood and walked out to the hall, I heard him lift the receiver and could hear his voice but not make out the words. Whether it was still my confused state muffling my ears or whether he was keeping his voice low, I didn't know.

Stepping back into the room he said, "They're on their way."

***

Thirty minutes later a confident knock at the front door finally kick-started my heart into action. It started at a slow beat, gradually becoming fast and hard as the two burly policemen stepped into the room.

The younger one, his face young and fresh sat at the far end of the settee next to Luke. The older one, who introduced himself as Sergeant Walker settled into Mum's chair, leaving her to stand next to me.

"Now, I understand the missing girl, Rebecca Summers came here on Monday night. Can you tell me what happened that evening?" Sergeant Walker asked, his voice deep and commanding.

I looked up to answer and saw him reel. His spine straightened and he actually jerked back in his seat, his mouth wide. Seeing his reaction the younger officer followed his gaze and stared at me, like I was a mirage or something.

"Rebecca?" Sergeant Walker finally managed.

Shaking my head I said, "No, I'm Rachel."

"Rachel and Rebecca are identical twins," Mum explained.

The officers shared a knowing look but it was the grey-haired Sergeant who spoke.

"Rebecca's mother mentioned a twin sister who made contact earlier this year. She said the pair of you stayed in Scarborough during the summer with your …" He consulted his notebook. "Your gran but said there was no current communication between you."

"Rebecca's mum and dad argue about her adoption and about me so she doesn't tell them when she's coming here," I said, quietly, hoping I wasn't getting Rebecca in trouble. But then, how could I make things worse than they already were? "Her parents are trying to get back together so Rebecca thought it best to let them think we aren't seeing each other. She usually says she's going to a friend's. Which is true, isn't it?"

Sergeant Walker shook his head with a sigh.

"Mrs Summers had no contact details for you and there was nothing in Rebecca's room to indicate an ongoing relationship. We have therefore initially concentrated on the immediate family, friends and neighbourhood. That has now cost us precious time. Why did you wait so long to contact us?"

"I didn't know she was missing!" I couldn't believe this. He was saying that if anything bad happened to Rebecca it was my fault!

Sitting forward in his chair, the older officer's eyes trawled over my face, as though my features could reveal some clue.

"So, what happened when Miss Summers was here? Did you argue at all?" he said, at last.

"No!" I almost shouted. He really was blaming me. "I've been having some trouble at school and Rebecca said I could switch to her school. We talked about that."

"And what did you decide?"

"I didn't, not then. I've thought about it since and decided to go there, but Rebecca doesn't know. I've been texting her," I finished quietly.

"So when did you last see her?"

"She left here at," I looked at the clock, like it'd still be on the same time or something, "Er, I think it was about, five o'clock. She walked down the drive. I waved goodbye."

The realisation that the goodbye might have been our last, suddenly hit me like a force field. Anything could've happened to her. I might never see her again. My eyes stung, as through the window behind Sergeant Walker, I saw Mr Shepherd walking his Labrador, Blacky. The image blurred as I remembered the last time I'd been in this state watching him walk by, I'd just found out I was adopted. Now my brand new twin sister was missing.

"Will you get her back?" I asked, wiping the tears away with the palm of my hand.

"We will do our best," he replied. "Was there anyone else present when Rebecca visited?"

"I was here," Mum said.

"So was I, later on," Dad added.

"And she left alone?"

"Yes." I answered.

The officer frowned. "This trouble at school, would anyone hurt Rebecca thinking she was you?"

I looked at Luke who shrugged, shaking his head.

"I don't think so," I said, hesitantly. "No," I added more firmly. "I've been at school for the last two days and Emma hasn't looked a bit surprised or anything. Anyway, she's mean but she's not violent. Well, not *that* violent."

I looked up at the officer, "You don't think she's been hurt, do you?"

"I'm afraid at this stage we don't know anything but we're still optimistic."

He asked loads more questions before finally looking up at Mum, then Dad. "Do you think Rachel could help us?"

I sat up. Never mind asking them, whatever it was, I'd help.

"In what way?" Mum asked, her voice hesitant.

"Usually, in these cases we do a reconstruction of the victi …. Eh, erm, missing person's last movements. In Rachel we have the best look-alike we're ever likely to get. Chances are, if Rachel could do a reconstruction, people's memories may be jogged."

Mum frowned, her hand raising and resting on her mouth. I glanced at Dad, his head was shaking ever so slightly.

"Yes, I'll do it!" I said, firmly. There was no way Mum and Dad were gonna stop me helping Rebecca.

"Rachel, it could be dangerous," Mum said, giving me the 'I need to wrap you in cotton wool' look.

"How? I'm only going to walk down the road, there'll be cameras and police and everything. Won't there?" I turned to the officers who nodded in unison.

"That's right, Mrs Brooks," Sergeant Walker said, "Your daughter will be perfectly safe."

"Can you be certain of that?" Dad asked.

"Yes, it's only a reconstruction."

Dad sighed. "Very well."

"Michael?" Mum frowned at Dad.

"It's all right, Love, she'll be well looked after."

"I'll be okay, Mum," I said, looking up at her worried face and trying to send rays of confidence to her. Trouble was, I didn't have that much confidence myself so infusing any into Mum wasn't easy.

Finally she nodded and I looked eagerly at the officers.

"When do we do it?"

***

"Are you sure about this?" Luke asked, two hours later.

Standing at the bottom of our drive, we watched as the film crew unloaded their equipment from a shiny white van. Several neighbours peered through windows or stood gawking in the street.

Trying to stop my stomach jumping like a kid skipping rope, I nodded.

"Hmm," was all I could manage.

"You can still back out."

I shook my head, "No way, I'm doing this for Rebecca. Just thinking about her being missing and what could be happening to her …" I looked up at him. "Luke, what if she's already dead?"

Luke's gaze intensified and he took hold of my shoulders. "Don't even think like that, you've got to believe she's alive and this is gonna help."

"I'm scared for her, Luke." My bottom lip trembled and I could feel my eyes stinging. "Where is she?"

Luke's arms wrapped tightly around me drawing me in to him. "I don't know," he whispered into my hair, "I wish I did."

"Are you all right, Miss?" asked the young officer who I now knew as Officer McKenzie.

I nodded, blinking hard and rubbing my eyes.

Officer McKenzie's eyes softened. "I know this can't be easy for you, Rachel, but you are doing the right thing and hopefully this will help us get Rebecca back. Normally we'd give you a little more preparation time, but as she's already been missing two days... Are you ready?"

I nodded.

"Now, just start here and do exactly what Rebecca did on Monday evening."

I nodded again, taking a deep breath and wishing I didn't feel so sick. Luke squeezed my hand and gave me a reassuring smile before joining Officer McKenzie behind the camera. I closed my eyes, breathing deeply to try and settle my racing heart, then opening them again I turned back towards the house and waved.

"Bye!" I shouted, before turning right and walking down the road. The cameraman followed on my left making me want to fidget. I'd never felt so self-conscious in all my life. It even topped my first day at Riverside Comp. I was sure I was walking like a total wally, partly because of nerves and partly because I couldn't get the image of Rebecca taking the very same steps the last time I saw her. A sob caught in my throat and I swallowed hard.

Stop thinking, Rachel, I commanded myself, *just do it*.

They followed me down the road and around the corner then stopped. I didn't have to walk all the way to the bus station because they didn't know whether Rebecca had made it that far. They had me do it a second time to be sure, then packed up and left.

I watched their van turn the corner then said goodbye to Officer McKenzie who told me I'd done a great job. Walking back into the house, I felt empty. I flopped down on the settee and Luke dropped down beside me.

"I'll make you a cuppa," Mum said, disappearing into the kitchen.

"You okay, Rachel, Love?" Dad asked.

I nodded.

Dad looked from me to Luke then left the room. Sometimes Dad could actually figure out what I wanted.

I leaned across and snuggled into Luke's chest. I could hear his heart beating and feel the vibration as he spoke.

"You did good, Rach."

"You think?"

"Yeah. I reckon it'll really help them find Rebecca."

I knew he was only saying it to make me feel better but I loved him for it. Squeezing him tighter I stayed snuggled in, not even moving when Mum brought the cuppa.

***

I didn't sleep at all that night and every limb ached as I walked to school the next day. My insides felt totally empty, like there was no life in me at all.

School was like a wall of silence, nobody said a word to me, but everybody stared. Some opened their mouths like they wanted to speak then clamped them shut again. I'd no idea whether they were still too scared of Emma or whether they just didn't know what to say to somebody whose sister was missing.

Even when I joined Becca and Luke at break and lunch it didn't cheer me up. Becca would be gone by the weekend and I couldn't monopolise all of Luke's time, he had to mix with his friends. I was so down I didn't even have the energy to worry about Emma. Whenever we passed or shared lessons, she just smiled triumphantly at me. I suppose Rebecca disappearing was a huge joy to Emma. I mean, Rebecca wasn't exactly polite to her the last time they met. Seeing me miserable wasn't gonna upset her either, in fact it was probably the highlight of her week.

I tried ringing Rebecca all day but it just kept going to her voicemail and every time my mood just sank lower and lower.

By the end of the day, I felt totally drained and it was then that Carly decided to strike.

I'd just left the school building and only had to cross to the gates before escaping for the day, but no such luck. Carly's voice wheedled in my ear.

"So, the twin's disappeared? Great, one less mini psycho."

Ignore her Rachel, my brain screamed.

"What, nothing to say? Come on, stop pretending to be calm, you know you want to have a go at me, it's in your blood."

58

She followed me across the tarmac, stepping sideways on my left like a crab. Why did Luke have to have football practice today of all days? Even Becca had stayed behind to say goodbye to some teachers she wouldn't see tomorrow.

"Just shut it, Carly!" I hissed and immediately wished I hadn't. I'd responded which was exactly what she wanted.

"Ooh, hostile. Got some of those nasty violent genes flaring up inside you?" Carly goaded. "I say it's a good thing that twin of yours is gone. We'll all be safer. I hope she's dead …"

She didn't get any further because all my resolve left me. In one move I spun around and pushed the much bigger Carly as hard as I could back against the huge waste bins.

"I said, 'shut it'," I hissed. "You hear me? My sister's missing, anything could've happened to her and you're nothing but a cowardly worm, you're not even good enough to say her name. You understand? I don't want to hear you say another word about her."

My heart was pounding so hard and fast it felt like a kick boxer inside my chest. Carly's face was a picture of panic, she'd lost several degrees of colour even her lips were white. Her hands were raised and trembling, unsure whether to submit, defend herself or actually go on the offensive. I was about to let go, I'd made my point, way more than I'd planned, when Carly's face changed. The look of shock slowly slid away and was replaced by a smile that grew into an assured grin with every nanosecond. As her body stiffened and straightened into a confident stance, I knew what had happened. I knew that if I turned now, Emma would be right behind me.

Carly's hands swept in, thrusting sharply against my shoulders pushing me away.

"It's such a shame. I'm so sorry for you, Rachel. You just can't help yourself. It's in the genes." Emma's smooth voice spread out like tar and I knew she had an audience who were sticking to those tacky words like flies in a web. It was the end of school, everybody was leaving the building and I'd just put on the perfect display to prove my enemies right.

"She's a total psychopath like the rest of her birth family," Carly snarled. "She probably did her twin in. I bet they argued. Rebecca said something she didn't like and Rachel went for her, just like she did with me."

My fists clenched as I stuck my face within centimeters of hers.

"Well if that's the case, Carly, I'd be careful if I were you. Who knows what could happen to you on a dark night when nobody's around?" I looked at Emma, "And that goes for you too. You can't have your little army with you all the time. I might just sneak up behind you with a kitchen knife and bury you where you'll never be found!" I spun around, my eyes scanning the crowd of nosy onlookers. "And that goes for the rest of you. If you want to cause me trouble or make jokes about my sister, you go ahead, but you'd better look behind you from now on!"

With that, I pushed my way past Carly and Emma, through the crowd and out of school, hearing their voices raised behind me.

"She just threatened us."

"We should tell the head."

"Didn't I tell you?" Emma's voice was triumphant, "None of us are safe."

60

Way to go, Rach. Now you've really done it.
My face and eyes burned all the way home and I bit my bottom lip to stop it trembling. I'd just made everything *so* much worse. I couldn't believe how gullible they all were, believing Emma. Who'd have thought on my first day back in April that shy, quiet Becca would be the only one to stand with me against everybody else.

And now Becca was leaving. With Luke's practices I was gonna be on my own so much it'd be open season on me for the likes of Emma and Carly. Even the chance of switching schools had disappeared along with Rebecca.

Just thinking about Rebecca sent another painful stab through my heart and when I reached home, I flopped down on the settee totally exhausted. Picking up the remote, I switched the TV on and stared at it without really watching until Luke arrived. Mum let him in and he settled onto the settee beside me.

"I heard," he said softly, as I snuggled in to him. He flicked the TV off and draped his arm across my shoulders. "I'm sorry I wasn't there."

"You can't be there all the time," I murmured, the sadness in me so strong it seemed to seep through my pores like garlic. "I'm so fed up, Luke. When will it all end?"

"I don't know, I wish I did."

Talking quietly, I wasn't even aware that I'd nodded off until the sound of the television woke me.

Luke rubbed his arm as I straightened up.

"Sorry," I murmured, blinking to get my eyes to focus.

Dad was home and sitting forward in his chair, staring at the TV like it was going to issue orders. Mum sat in her chair opposite with the television on her left, looking sort of shrunken like she was afraid the TV would bite her.

"Have I been asleep long?" I asked, yawning.

"Only about twenty minutes," Luke answered. But then our conversation ended as Rebecca's face appeared on screen behind the female news reader.

"Last Monday Rebecca Summers left the house of her twin sister, Rachel Brooks. As seen here," my reconstruction appeared, "Re-enacted by her sister Rachel. Rebecca walked happily down the road towards Rotherham Central Bus Station and has not been seen since. Abandoned as infants, Rachel and Rebecca were adopted separately and were only re-united earlier this year after an extensive search by tenacious Rachel."

Tenacious, me?

"In this tragic turn of events they are separated once more by the disappearance of Rebecca. By doing the reconstruction Rachel is once again attempting to find her missing twin. If anyone has any news of Rebecca's whereabouts or remembers seeing her on Monday please contact the police on the number below."

Another news story came up and Dad pressed the remote, plunging the room into silence.

Mum sighed heavily. I still sat there, staring at the blank screen, silently begging someone to ring.

***

CHAPTER SEVEN

"Any news?"

Luke watched me intently as I walked down the drive the next morning. I shook my head.

"I haven't heard anything but then they'd contact Rebecca's parents rather than us. I've asked Mum if we can go round there tonight after school."

Luke's eyebrows raised. "You think that's a good idea?"

Shrugging, I joined him on the pavement and we set off towards school.

"I don't see how it can do any harm. I mean, they now know where she was on Monday. They'll probably want to know what we were talking about."

"But it was only about you changing schools. That's got nothing to do with what happened to Rebecca."

"I know, but I was thinking if I was the one missing, Mum and Dad would want to know every tiny detail, no matter how irrelevant. Don't you think?"

Now it was Luke's turn to shrug.

"I don't know, Rach. I haven't a clue about any of this."

As we rounded the corner and school came into sight Luke looked down at me. "Are you going to be okay today?"

Looking ahead at the huge gates and everybody heading in, my stomach actually managed to tighten further than it had already.

"Not much choice," I said, my voice flat.

"Well try and stay away from Emma and Carly," he instructed.

"I didn't exactly go looking for them yesterday," I snapped.

"Whoa! Just trying to help." Luke held up his hands in mock surrender.

"Sorry." I grimaced. "I guess I'm just real stressed."

"It's okay," Luke said, with a smile. "I'll survive."

My boyfriend is totally the best!

We'd reached the school grounds and started across the tarmac. Everybody we passed stared and it was definitely not my imagination. I felt like I'd grown two heads or something. Luke's arm tightened around me and didn't let go until we were in school.

"Don't let them get to you," he whispered before heading off in the opposite direction for his class.

I walked down the hall with everybody's eyes on me. If this was how it felt to be famous I didn't want it. I'd rather be totally anonymous.

"Rachel." A girl from my Math's class stepped out of the passing crowd into my path. She'd never spoken to me since my argument with Emma back in April.

Here we go, I thought and waited for her to verbally lay into me.

"I'm sorry about what's happened to your twin," she began. "It's awful, I hope they find her."

Wow, that was unexpected.

"Er, thanks," I said.

"And I think you're real brave going on TV like that."

"Thanks," I said again as she nodded then headed off down the corridor and was swallowed up by the teaming mass of students heading for their classes. But hers wasn't the only surprise. During the day at least ten other people stopped me to say sorry about Rebecca and mentioned my appearance on TV. Maybe they wanted a claim to fame, or maybe it was genuine. I'd no idea but it was loads better than having people snipe at me all day.

"Will you come by my house tomorrow?" Becca asked as we walked part of the way home together.

I wasn't really up to sad goodbyes but there wasn't exactly much option, so I nodded.

"Yeah, what time are you setting off?"

"About three thirty." Becca's eyes were filling just at the thought of it and I could feel mine doing the same.

"I wish you could come round tonight," I said.

"Yeah, me too, but there's still loads to pack."

"Okay, I'll come round for three o'clock."

Becca's smile was weak. "Thanks Rach."

We'd reached the end of the street where Becca turned off.

"See you tomorrow," she said.

"Yeah, see you," I said before hurrying off home. Tonight I was gonna meet Rebecca's parents and my nerves were already twitching.

***

As Dad turned onto Queen Street in Swinton, my stomach flipped right over like a pancake being tossed. I watched the Butcher's Arms pub slip by on our right then the Junior & Infant school and row of new houses before Dad pulled up on the left outside Rebecca's. Even though Mum had rung ahead to check whether it was okay for us to come, I still couldn't help nerves pricking my skin like a thousand needles.

Rebecca's mum must have been watching for us because the door swung open before we'd even stepped onto their small patch of front garden.

"Hello, please come in," she said, opening the door wide. Her face was a sickly grey, narrow and strained. As I stepped up behind Mum her eyes fixed on me and held. Even over the sound of passing cars I heard her sharp intake of breath.

We stood in the narrow hall, its red and brown linoleum hiding any sign of footprints or dirt. Mrs Summers closed the door then led the way into the lounge on her left.

The layout was amazingly like ours with a brown leather settee along the left wall, a single easy chair under the window and one directly ahead near the door. A wide screen TV dominated the wall opposite with an electric fire beneath.

Mr Summers sat in the chair nearest the door and looked up as we entered. His black hair was flecked with grey and he wore the same strained look as his wife. His eyes fixed on me too and as I lowered myself onto the settee I tried to sink as far into the corner as I could. Both Rebecca's parents were nicely dressed but everything hung loose like they'd been on a mega diet.

"You're her double." Mr Summer's voice sounded strangled.

Mrs Summers sat in the chair beneath the window shaking her head. "Rebecca said you were identical but I'd never … you're so alike!" Her voice was awed, like a child seeing snow for the first time.

"I didn't want Rebecca to find you," Mr Summer's shot an accusing glance at his ex-wife.

"It was me who found her," I said quickly, not wanting them to start one of their renowned arguements. They'd been trying to get back together before Rebecca vanished; I wondered whether that'd ever happen now. "I'm sorry. I just wanted to find my birth family."

"And now Rebecca's missing," Mr Summers said, the implication plain, his eyes fierce.

"Now, wait a minute!" my dad jumped in. "That's not my Rachel's fault. We don't know what happened to your daughter but we're here to see if there's anything we can do to help."

Mr Summers deflated a bit. "I'm sorry. Right now I'm ready to blame anybody." He looked at me. "I'm sorry, Rachel. I just want my daughter back."

His voice was so flat. My throat tightened and I could feel tears building behind my eyes. What if this was my fault? What if Rebecca was gone because she'd come to see me? I mean, she wouldn't have been in Rotherham if I'd done what my parents asked and left her alone.

"I'm sorry," I whispered, then bit my lip real quick to stop a sob escaping.

Mum's hand rested on mine, her right leg pressed against my left. Any further and she'd have been on my knee.

"It's alright, Sweetheart," she said. "Everything will be okay."

I couldn't help remembering my first day at Riverside Comp. That's what Mum said then and look how that turned out.

"Can you tell us what happened on Monday?" Mrs Summers asked, her voice barely more than a whisper.

I shrugged. "There's not a lot to tell, really. Rebecca's been coming over every couple of weeks or so, but Monday we were talking about me maybe going to her school."

"Why's that?" Mr Summers sat up like this could be of major importance.

"I'm having some problems at school and was thinking about getting away." I told them all about Emma, Carly, Luke and Becca. They nodded and asked questions but by the end Mr Summers was frowning.

"This Emma and Carly, just how far would they go to get at you?"

"They wouldn't go this far!" I jumped in then mentally pulled myself back. Did I really know that? "At least, I don't think they would, but Luke didn't turn Emma down until Wednesday so it can't be them."

"Hmn," Mr Summers huffed.

"Rachel, I hadn't realised it had become this serious at school. Why didn't you tell me?" Mum twisted to face me, her forehead all puckered. "I could have spoken to your head teacher."

"I wanted to handle it myself," I said. *So much for not telling Mum about it all.*

The front door opened and closed. Footsteps advanced down the hall, reaching the lounge door.

"Who are they?" The voice was deep and had a sort of 'fed up' note.

I turned in my seat to see a boy, about eighteen, with torn hipster jeans, blue hoody and three silver ear rings in each ear.   He gasped when he saw me and dropped down to stare just centimeters from my face.

"No way!" His head twisted as he looked at me from every angle. "You've got to be Rachel."

"Liam, don't be so rude!" Mrs Summer's said, her voice stronger now.

"Yeah, right." Liam stood again, still staring at me. "So you're the twin? You here to help get Rebecca back?"

"Erm, yeah." I said. *Like, how?*

For a moment Liam's gaze was intense, like he was trying to read my soul then he nodded, spun around and left the room.

"Sorry about that," Mrs Summers said. "He's a teenager. He's getting better."

Like it was some sort of disease or something.

My mobile vibrated in my bag and I looked around apologetically.

"It's all right, go ahead," Mr Summers said with a nod.

"Hello, Rachel, I saw you on the news last night! Why didn't you tell me about Rebecca?"

Glancing around nervously, I tried to figure out what to say without letting on that Marcy was on the phone. If Mr Summers didn't like Rebecca knowing and visiting me, he'd totally flip out at the thought of our birth mother being in touch.

"Er, I've been a bit busy."

"Busy! Rachel, this is my daughter we're talking about! How can you not think to tell me?"

"Well, you're not, er, exactly in touch."

"That's not my choice." She sounded wounded. "You know that. Rebecca said she didn't want contact with me and I respect that. But that's not the point. She's missing. I have a right to know."

I wanted to shout, '*No you don't! You gave up that right when you dumped us!*' I mean, I know why she gave us up and all that but just because I'd forgiven her didn't mean that what she did was okay. There were loads more options open to her without leaving us on a hospital door step one year apart. But I didn't say that. Instead I clenched my teeth and said, as calmly as I could.

"I'm sorry, I should've rung. But look, I'm busy right now. I'll ring you later."

"Busy? Rachel, this is important! I need you to tell me …."

I didn't hear any more because I did what I've never done before, I hung up on her.

"Who was that, Rachel?" Dad asked from the far end of the sofa.

I saw the look of panic cross Mum's face. She'd been near enough to hear some of what Marcy said and knew who it was.

"It doesn't matter, right now," she said.

"Well, it sounded important," Dad persisted.

"It was nothing, Dad," I said.

I purposely looked across at Rebecca's dad to try and resume the conversation but his eyes were narrowed.

"Who was that, Rachel?" he asked, his voice quiet but suspicious.

"A friend," I lied, I mean, what was I supposed to say?

Mr Summers' lips tightened until they were just narrow lines.

"I heard her say that Rebecca is her daughter. Or did I hear wrong?"

"Darren," Mrs Summers cautioned.

"No, Ruth, I heard most of that conversation. It wasn't a child, it was a woman and she was shouting. She said that Rebecca is her daughter. So Rachel, just who were you talking to?"

Swallowing, I tried to find a way out but there was none. I looked down at the mobile still in my hand.

"It was Marcy Phelps," I croaked. "Mine and Rebecca's birth mother."

Mrs Summers gasped and sat like a statue, a hand over her mouth while Mr Summer's cheeks slowly turned red and I waited for the explosion.

"Just when did Rebecca have contact with *her*?" He spat out the final word, turning his accusing eyes on his wife.

"I, I didn't know she had," Mrs Summers moved her hand just enough to speak.

"Mrs Summers didn't know," I said, quietly, still staring down at the phone. "Marcy saw us in Scarborough. Rebecca didn't want to see her and sent her away. She hasn't had any other contact. I'm the only one in touch with her."

Right then I was so glad I'd already told Mum and Dad about Marcy. I couldn't have dealt with four pairs of accusing eyes. Two were enough.

"And you didn't think this was important?" Mr Summers' voice sounded strangled and I finally looked up to see his face, now a shade of purple. He looked like an over-ripe plum that was about to pop.

"It isn't. Rebecca hasn't had any contact with her," I whispered.

"All the more reason to make her a suspect!" Mr Summers jumped to his feet. I guess holding it in was no longer an option.

My 'why?' must have shown on my face because he raged on.

71

"My Rebecca rejected her! She's this warped woman who abandoned her kids years ago! She's obviously not right in her head. Then after only a few months of coming back into your lives, my Rebecca disappears! How not relevant is that? Rebecca rejected her! She's probably flipped out and abducted her! I can't believe I'm only hearing about this now!"

"But Marcy wanted to meet her, that's all. She's okay, she'd not hurt her," I said, weakly.

"And how do you know that? You've only just met the woman, you know nothing about her!" Spit spattered in drops from his lips as he raged.

"Now, look, there's no need for this. Just calm down," my dad soothed. His voice sounded strained like it was all he could do to keep from shouting in my defense.

"No need? You knew about this, didn't you? What kind of parent are you to not bring this up?"

"Hey, now, I'm a good father. At least my daughter felt she could tell me about this which is more than your daughter could." Dad was on his feet now. This was getting way out of hand.

Both mothers just sat there. Mrs Summers so white she looked like she'd pass out. My mum's grip on my hand had tightened so much it was actually hurting.

"What's going on?" a sullen but curious voice asked from the doorway. I didn't need to look to know that Liam had come to investigate the raised voices.

"Are you calling me a bad father?" Mr Summers yelled, ignoring his son.

"No!" My dad's voice went up a notch as well, "And I'm not one either. This is hard for everybody."

"Oh, so I'm not coping now, *is that it*?"

72

I could feel every organ in my body tightening. This wasn't helping Rebecca.

Both Dad and Mr Summers took a step towards one another, their fists clenched.

"Stop it! Stop it, now!" Jumping up, I stood between them, terrified they were gonna fight. "This isn't helping," I said more softly, twisting to look at each in turn.

Both men stared at me, then at Mum and Mrs Summers like they'd woken up from a nightmare and didn't know where they were.

"Oh, er, I'm sorry," my dad gasped and used the back of his hand to wipe away the sweat beneath his brown fringe. "I guess we got carried away."

Mr Summers' Adam's apple bobbed as he swallowed hard. "Erm, yes, emotions are running high. I'm sorry too." He backed away towards his chair as Dad dropped onto the settee.

I let out a long breath and sank back down beside Mum.

"We have to inform the police," Mr Summers said, quietly now. He looked at me. "It may be nothing, but they have to follow up any possible angles and this is definitely something they need to know."

I nodded. I still didn't fully get it. I mean, I knew Marcy, she was all meek and frightened, not the sort of person who'd hurt anybody. But like Mr Summers said, what did I know? I'd only met her a couple of months ago and all I knew was what she'd told me. She could've told me a pack of lies. I mean, look at Mark. He was like, totally gone.

"Is Mark still in prison?" I asked in a whisper.

"He will be darling," my mum said, tapping my leg, "He won't be out for some time."

"He might have got bail."

Mr Summers' head tilted, "And Mark is … ?"

"The one who attacked me, Rebecca and Gran." I paused. He was *so* not gonna like this. "He's our birth brother."

Mr Summers sucked in most of the air in the room, but managed to keep his cool this time. Rebecca had told them about the attack but not the family connection.

"He's still in prison," Mrs Summers said, quietly. "I didn't know about the *family* connection, but I did mention the attack to the police and they said he was still inside."

"I'm going to ring the police now," Mr Summers said, his voice cracking with strain. "What's this Marcy's address?"

Reluctantly I told him, feeling like an informant. I mean, she was my birth mother and I'd all but turned her in for Rebecca's kidnapping when she probably had nothing to do with it.

He headed out into the hall and I heard his feet pad upstairs. He obviously didn't want us listening in. We all sat in silence like a sentence had been passed and nobody knew what to do about it. Finally his feet padded back downstairs, a squeaky floor board letting us know he was near the bottom.

"Okay," he said, "The police were very interested to know about Marcy. They're going to see her and ask her a few questions." He held out a piece of paper with a name and number scrawled on it. "That's the number for Sergeant Holmes. Ring him if you think of anything else they need to know."

My throat tightened. The police were gonna interrogate Marcy. I felt like such a low life telling on her. I mean, from her phone call, she didn't know anything about it but because of me she could be in loads of trouble. I'd seen enough T.V. shows to know that when something happens in a family you're guilty until proven innocent and Marcy did abandon us as babies. I looked at Dad, silently pleading with him to get me out of this. Reaching out, he took the paper from me.

"I'll ring them if we think of anything." He looked at me. "You can tell Marcy you didn't have any choice. It wasn't your fault she rang while you were here."

I nodded, my throat still feeling like it was stuck together on the inside.

"I don't think there's anything else we can do right now," Dad said, standing and extending his hand to Mr Summers. "I'll give you our number and you can ring if there's anything we can do to help."

Mr Summers' grip looked firm as he shook Dad's hand. "Thank you for coming we appreciate it and I'm sorry about ...."

Dad shook his head. "Don't worry about it you're under a great deal of stress. I can't imagine how I'd feel if ..." He glanced at me.

Mr Summers nodded as the rest of us stood. Mrs Summers cut through every one to stand in front of me. Her eyes raked slowly over me then suddenly her arms were around me squeezing so tight I could hardly breathe.

"Look after yourself, Rachel," she whispered. "And if there's anything you can remember, anything at all, you get in touch with us, you hear?"

She stopped hugging but still held me at arm's length. Her eyes damp. "You're so alike. We have to get her back. We have to get my Rebecca back."

Her mouth twisted as her eyes filled with tears.

"We will," I said, my own eyes stinging. "We have to."

And then, maybe because I didn't really believe it was possible, I twisted out of her grip and headed for the door.

"We've got to go," I said, my voice already shaking.

"Er, yes, we'll be in touch." The tone of Mum's voice told me she'd picked up my mood and within seconds she was walking me down the hall, her hand on my back. Her touch was enough, to start the tears, I couldn't stop them anymore. Mum didn't wait for the Summers to open the door. She opened it herself and ushered me down the steps to our car, keeping me facing away from the house.

Dad was moments behind us, shouting 'goodbye' for us all. He plipped the car open and I gratefully climbed in the back. I saw Mum wave as we pulled out, but I couldn't. Staring down at my lap I didn't look at anything else until we were well and truly away from their house.

"Are you okay, Love?" Mum asked, trying to twist in her seat.

Shaking my head, I sniffed and reached for a tissue from the box on the back shelf.

"What if I never see her again, Mum?" I asked, wiping my nose. "We've only just found each other. What if that's it? What if she's … "

I knew the next word but it caught in my throat. I couldn't say it.

"I wish I could tell you it's not so, Honey, but I can't," Mum said, as Dad turned onto Warren Vale Road. Trees stood to attention on either side, orange, green and brown like soldiers on guard. If only someone had guarded Rebecca. "But we're not giving up hope. There's every chance she's still aliv … er …okay."

Somehow Mum trying to avoid the obvious word made it worse and I just cried harder. The tears wouldn't stop. There was no avoiding it. Rebecca was gone and might even be dead already. I might never see her again. Ever.

By the time we reached home I was shaking all over. Mum bundled me in, pushed me down onto the settee and headed into the kitchen. I heard the tap run then the kettle switch on. Mum's answer to everything. A sweet drink of tea. I didn't even like tea but seemed to be drinking loads of it lately.

Dad hovered near the lounge door then backed away into the kitchen. I could hear him and Mum whispering.

Closing my eyes I tried to blot out reality, but it didn't work. Images of Rebecca waving goodbye flashed in my mind. Then Rebecca being forced into a car, screaming for help but no one came. My eyes shot open.

"Here, drink this." Mum held out a steaming mug in front of me. I took it but just stared into the brown liquid.

"Your mum and I have been talking," Dad said. "I think you should stay in this weekend and your Mum will walk you to school next week."

"But Luke walks me." Those few minutes totally alone with my boyfriend were precious to me, the idea of Mum intruding was unthinkable.

Mum looked at Dad and nodded.

"Alright, Luke can walk you to school, but you are not to be alone at any time. If Luke has practice then Mum or I collect you. Okay?"

"But why?"

"Look Rachel." Dad's voice was firm. "We don't know who took Rebecca or why, but it was from near here. He could still be around."

My heart tripped over.

"You think whoever it was might come for me?" A shiver traveled through my whole body like a ghost had passed through.

"No!" Dad's answer was too quick, "It's just, well, it's just the sensible thing to do. We have to know you're safe."

"So you do think he'll come for me? Or did he want me in the first place? Did Rebecca get taken instead of me?"

Suddenly I couldn't breathe. My hands shook and I saw the cup tilt. Tea spilled out before the cup slid completely from my hands.

"Oh, Rachel!" Mum rushed forwards, snatched up the cup and hurried out to the kitchen.

Dad came over and sat next to me on the settee, placing his hand on mine.

"Rachel. We don't know anything. We don't know why Rebecca was taken, but right now we have to take every possibility into account and make sure you're safe until he's caught."

"But it could be weeks or months or …" My words fizzled out and I couldn't complete the sentence. I couldn't imagine not getting Rebecca back for that long. I swallowed hard, breathing wasn't getting any easier. "You can't follow me around forever," I whispered.

"We'll follow you for as long as it takes." Mum was back. She dropped to her knees and started mopping up my mess.

"But I'll be a prisoner." Maybe Rebecca already was. "I have to go say goodbye to Becca

78

tomorrow," I said, quietly. This all felt like a nightmare. I wanted to wake up and find myself back at home in Scarborough, before all this. But then there'd be no Luke and no Rebecca. I couldn't lose them. My head dropped into my hands, there was just no way out.

"Don't worry, Love. Your dad will run you over there. He'll wait then bring you back." Mum's voice was sympathetic but firm and I knew there was no point arguing.

Suddenly I saw a future permanently guarded, under house arrest with no friends, except Luke. What kind of life was that?

"What am I going to do, Dad?" I sobbed as tears fell again.

"Don't worry, Honey, we'll look after you," he assured. "You'll be okay."

But I knew there was no way he could guarantee that. No one could.

***

CHAPTER EIGHT

My heart squeezed tight as Dad's car turned onto Becca's street and the removal van came into sight. Beds, chairs and boxes closely packed like lego blocks almost reached the doors. Sadness built up inside me like thick liquid filling every space. I didn't want to get out of the car. I wanted to tell Dad to turn around so I could go away and pretend it wasn't happening.

"Rachel!" Becca came out of her front door, waving madly. There was no escape now. Heaving myself out of Dad's Vauxhall, I walked towards my friend. All the houses were huge and detached, their front lawns long and tidy. Even the street was wide like they needed more room for the bigger cars. Becca's parents were definitely loaded.

"How's it going?"

Becca shrugged. "We're leaving so much behind it feels like we're not really going until I walk into my room. All my stuff's already in the van." She sighed. "I liked that room."

"You okay?"

Becca shook her head. "I'm gonna miss you, Rach. You and Luke. Part of me doesn't want to leave you two and this house, but another part can't wait to get away from Emma and co. You know what I mean?"

"Yeah." I knew all too well. "I really hope it all works out for you."

Becca looked down at her feet, shuffling on the pavement.

"Any news about Rebecca?"

I shook my head.

"I'm real sorry to be going when all this is happening. You know I'd stay if I could?"

"Yeah, I know."

"I've got to get back in and help. You want to come in?"

I nodded and followed her back up her drive. I should have said more but was scared that if I said too much I'd just start bawling right there in the street. I felt like I was sinking into tarry blackness and didn't know how to get out. Any time soon I'd disappear, sucked under completely, but would anybody really notice?

By the time everything was loaded half hour later I felt almost submerged. I stood there on the pavement, waving at Becca's sad face as their Merc gradually shrunk into the distance behind the removal van.

Now there was only my adoptive parents and Luke on my side. Even my relationship with Mum and Dad wasn't the same.

I sank into the front seat beside Dad, wishing Luke was there, holding me, but I didn't text him. I didn't want Luke thinking I'd be too clingy without Becca.

As Dad turned into our drive, the first thing I saw was Luke sitting on the low garden wall.

"Luke!" I yelled, feeling the blackness lift a little.

As soon as the car stopped I flung the door open and sprinted across the grass. Flinging myself at him I felt an instant warmth as his arms enfolded me.

I heard Dad's footsteps retreating towards the house, leaving us alone.

My head tilted and our tongues met. I was desperate, like I needed to sap energy and security from him. Thankfully Luke didn't seem to mind as he kissed me just as vigorously. When we finally came up for air, we sat on the garden wall, our backs to the road and just hugged. I nestled into him as tightly as possible. Any closer and I'd have been inside his skin. He didn't ask if I was okay, he just held me.

We sat like that for ages until my mobile rang. I ignored it and let it go to voicemail, but then it rang again and again and again.

Rebecca. The thought sprang into my mind and I yanked the phone out of my bag without even looking at the display.

"Rebecca!" I cried.

"No, it's me." My heart didn't just sink, it plummeted to the bottom of my trainers. "Have you got anything you want to tell me, Rachel?"

"Marcy, I'm sorry," I gasped. "But I was in Rebecca's house when you rang and her dad went all ballistic when he knew it was you. He insisted on ringing the police. I'm so sorry. Did they come round?"

"Oh, yes, they came round." Marcy's voice was acidic. "They took me down to the station to 'help with their enquiries'. Do you know how scared I was? They kept me there all night. They wanted to know all about me abandoning you both, about Mark and Jed's violence. They wanted to know if I was angry with Rebecca because she doesn't want to know me. They treated me like some sort of criminal!" Her voice was rising, I could tell by Luke's raised eyebrows that he could hear every word. "You know what they did? They threatened to charge me under the Offences Against the Person Act for abandoning you both! I was saving your lives but that didn't matter to them."

My heart was already sprinting, beating fast because of her anger.

"They won't charge you, will they?"

"I've spoken to a solicitor friend of mine and he says he doesn't think so. It's very rare for them to do that but if Rebecca isn't found … They've got to feel like they've got somebody for something."

"Oh, Marcy, I'm so sorry," I said again. "I didn't mean for any of this to happen. If you'd only rung after I'd left their house…"

"It's all right, Rachel." Her voice was a bit calmer now. "I know it wasn't your fault, but I felt … I felt like a criminal and I've never felt that way before. It was like they really thought I'd hurt Rebecca. I'd never hurt my own daughter."

No, but you could abandon us, my mind accused.

"I've booked a room at the Brentwood Hotel and I'm coming down," Marcy continued. "I feel so hopeless up here. I've got to be there and do something."

"I'm not sure there's anything you can do," I said, wishing she'd change her mind. I mean, neither of our adoptive families were exactly thrilled we were even in touch. Having her here would go down like a thunderstorm on sports day.

83

"There may not be, but I'm coming. I've taken leave from work and I'll be on a train in a couple of hours. I can't just sit by and do nothing, Rachel."

"Okay," I said.

After the call was ended I looked up at Luke.

"I think everything just got way more complicated," I said.

***

Luke was having a late tea with us when a knock at the front door made my last carrot stick in my throat. Looking across the kitchen table at Luke, I could see he was thinking the same as me. There had been just enough time for Marcy to travel from Scarborough, drop off her bags and arrive at my house.

"I'll go," Dad said, sliding out of his chair. He'd already finished his dinner and had been relaxing with a cup of tea and an extended stomach.

Putting my head down, I focused on my remaining dinner hoping I was wrong. Surely Marcy wouldn't just turn up here? Muffled voices drifted down the hall, one definitely female.

I pushed a forkful of mashed potato into my mouth as Dad spoke, his voice strained.

"Rachel, you have a visitor."

I turned, knowing who'd be standing there.

"Hello, Marcy," I said.

If possible my birth mother's lined face looked older than ever, her brown eyes hollow.

Mum gasped. She knew I'd met Marcy in Scarborough over the summer but she'd never wanted to meet her. Marcy was from my past and Mum would prefer she stayed there.

"Hello, Rachel."

"We're just finishing dinner," Mum said, needlessly. Unless Marcy was blind the 95% cleared plates pretty much spoke for themselves.

"I'm sorry to intrude," Marcy said, her voice the gentle inoffensive one she'd used all summer. "Would you prefer me to wait outside?"

"No, it's okay," Mum said, remembering her manners. "We're near enough done here. We'll take our drinks into the lounge. Unless you want to talk to Rachel alone, that is?"

"Oh, no, that's fine."

Wow, parents are so obvious, Marcy didn't really want the family around but didn't want to cause trouble and Mum didn't want me talking to Marcy alone.

We all dutifully picked up our cups and followed Dad in a snake-like trail to the lounge. The air was so thick with tension that I reckon even a sneeze would've made the whole place explode.

I noticed Mum didn't offer Marcy a drink, she probably figured she'd miss summat if she stayed behind to make one.

Dad dropped into his usual chair and Marcy settled hesitantly into the chair opposite. Mum's intake of breath behind me was so sharp it was almost a hiss. Unknowingly, Marcy had taken Mum's place adding credence to Mum's insecurities.

As me and Luke settled onto the settee, Mum pushed in to sit stiffly between us, silently declaring, *'You might have my chair but this is my daughter'*. I couldn't believe they were silently fighting over possession of me. Talk about childish! Well, actually it was Mum. I don't think Marcy had a clue about the implications of her choice of seating. In fact, Marcy's hands were slowly wringing in her lap.

"I don't want to intrude," she began. "I just want to know what happened to my Min ... Rebecca and to see whether I can help."

She'd been about to call Rebecca, Minnie, the name she gave her at birth because she was so tiny. Millie and Minnie, that's who we were supposed to be, we sounded like a pair of cartoon characters. There was definitely an upside to being adopted.

I recited the events of the night Rebecca disappeared, leaving out most of the stuff about Emma and Carly. Marcy might be my birth mum but I didn't know her well enough to confide all my problems.

Marcy kept asking whether there was anything she could do, but there just wasn't.

Saying 'goodnight' at the door an hour later, her shoulders slumped, she seemed so disappointed, but I didn't know what she'd expected. She didn't even know Rebecca. At their one and only meeting Rebecca pretended to be me and told Marcy to take a hike, so she wasn't exactly going to be full of insightful ideas on how to find her. Still, I felt sorry for Marcy. She gave us up to protect us from her violent husband then spent the next fourteen years trying to find us again. Only a couple of months after succeeding in her search Rebecca was missing.

"She'll be okay," Luke said over my shoulder as she walked away.

"She seems so sad."

"She probably is, but there's nothing you can do about that. Don't get me wrong, you can feel sorry for her but you can't take away all that happened in the past. Right now it's about Rebecca, not Marcy."

I nodded, knowing he was right, but an ache still lodged in my chest for the woman who gave up her children because she loved them too much to keep them. Sighing, I turned to Luke and nuzzled up against him, taking comfort from his strength and warmth. It was such a pity that Marcy didn't have anybody like Luke in her life.

Later that night after Luke had gone home, I followed Mum into the kitchen.

"Are you okay, Mum?"

She shrugged. "I suppose I should be."

"What do you mean?"

"I have my daughter. But just seeing her, here in this house." Mum shook her head. "The longing in her eyes made me feel like a thief."

"She gave me up, Mum."

"Oh, I know and I kept telling myself that but it didn't help."

"Then she sat in your chair."

Mum's eyes widened.

I smiled. "Yeah, I noticed. You thought she was trying to take your place and claim me back."

"How did you know?"

I rolled my eyes. "It was like, so obvious! Mum, Marcy had no idea which was your chair. She just picked one that looked comfy where she could sit on her own."

Mum's shoulders sagged. "I'm a complete idiot, aren't I?"

"I might not have used those exact words." I paused then grinned. "Well actually, yes, I might."

"Come here." Mum signaled me in and stepping closer I let her wrap her arms around me. Before finding out I was adopted we used to hug a lot but since April the hugs had been rare. We were learning how to relate all over again. "Rachel. I know these last few months have been hard, but you are my daughter. Even if I'd given birth to you, I couldn't love you more. I know Marcy is your birth mum but I'm the one who brought you up and she can never replace that."

"Mum, I know, okay?"

"Okay."

"So, what are we having for supper?"

"Supper! You nearly ate the table cloth at tea time!"

"We don't have a table cloth."

"We probably did before you ate it."

I grimaced. But at least it was a sign Mum was back to her normal, slightly crazy, self.

***

Once in bed I texted Marcy and arranged to meet her the next day. She'd looked so dejected I just wanted to check she was okay. Boy, having two mums to worry about was real hard work. We arranged to meet at the hotel at 10 am. I texted Luke who agreed to go with me so Mum and Dad wouldn't insist on driving. I figured the less time the three of them spent together, the better.

Bad dreams haunted me that night. Someone was hurting Rebecca. She was screaming for my help. I raced around, searching everywhere, but couldn't find her. 'You found me before,' she accused, 'you can find me again'. Our brother Mark kept showing up, grinning and taunting me that he knew where she was but I'd never find her. Marcy tried talking to him but he pulled out a knife and she ran. Mum instantly popped up saying Marcy was a terrible mother who should have better control of her son. Within seconds Marcy re-appeared, arguing that she was an excellent mother. I tried to calm them down and tell them it didn't matter, that we just had to find Rebecca but neither would listen.

When my alarm went off the next morning I was actually happy. A night like that was exhausting.

I sat up and pulled my curtains aside to see a layer of crisp white frost covering the ground. Shivering, I climbed out of bed and pulled on a pair of jeans followed by a thick red jumper. If I was gonna be walking to see Marcy there was no way I was gonna be cold.

After breakfast I slipped on my trainers and added my black leather jacket before heading out. Cold air hit my face as I spotted Luke leaning against the wall at the bottom of our drive. His short leather jacket hung open and he didn't even look cold! We walked with one arm around each other all the way to Gerard Road. I was absolutely freezing and my hands were numb by the time we walked down tree-lined Moorgate Road. The wind whipped through the branches sending a bunch of dead leaves and dust in my face.

I was real glad when the Brentwood with its fancy trees came into sight. The square, brown-bricked building stood alone at the top of a short flight of stone steps. Luke waited at the bottom while I climbed up, dried leaves crunching beneath my feet.

Marcy must have been watching for me because the red door opened and she stepped out before I'd even reached it. She wore a long padded beige coat that made her thin frame actually look normal size.

"Shall we walk?" she asked, glancing at Luke.

I shrugged. I'd have preferred the warmth inside the hotel but I was there to cheer her up so figured I'd better go along with her. We set off, Luke walking a few steps behind to give us some privacy.

"I'm sorry about my mum, yesterday," I began, as we retraced our steps down Moorgate Road.

"It's understandable," Marcy said, her head hunched into her shoulders against the cold wind. "I could feel the vibes, but it was my fault. It wasn't very wise of me just to turn up like that. I suppose if the situation were reversed I'd feel the same."

"They'll be all right. It's just been a lot for them to deal with this year. You know, me finding out about my adoption and searching for my birth family. They'd only just got used to Rebecca when I met you in Scarborough and Mark tried to kill us. Now Rebecca's gone missing and you turn up." I stopped to look at Marcy. "It's a lot for them to take in."

Marcy nodded. "I only wanted to help but my being here isn't making things any better, is it?"

Way to go, Marcy, put me right on the spot why don't you?

"Well, it does make things awkward, but, erm, maybe there's some way you can help."

Marcy's eyes widened, her face eager like a kid expecting a present. "How? I'd do anything to help! We've got to get Rebecca back."

She like, wanted me to suggest something right then! I stared at a white van passing slowly behind her while trying to come up with a good suggestion.

"Erm, well, I don't know yet, but I'm sure there'll be summat. At least you're here if you're needed."

"Oh," Marcy visibly shrank, like a cake falling flat after leaving the oven. "Well, erm, okay. Let me know if you think of something. I really want to help."

"I know and I'm really grateful." I put on an encouraging smile and it seemed to work as Marcy grew a bit again.

We walked and chatted more, about Scarborough, Gran, nursing and school before heading back up to the Brentwood.

Marcy stood and talked for a few more minutes before heading inside.

"That was *way* tense," I said as we set off back down Moorgate Road again. By the time we'd finished there was gonna be a groove in the pavement. "I was so close to putting my foot in it the whole time."

"Sounded like she really wanted to help."

"Yeah, she does but instead she's just making everything awkward."

"Isn't there anything she can do?" Luke looked down at me, the familiar frown between his eyes as a white van passed us and pulled up further down the road. Its heavy driver climbed out, walked around the front and stood looking down at the passenger side tyres.

"Beats me." I shook my head. "I don't even know what I can do. I just wish there was something. I feel so useless just walking around trying to keep everybody happy while Rebecca is somewhere, maybe hurt and waiting to be rescued. She might even be ..."

I couldn't finish the sentence. I still couldn't let myself think that it may be too late already.

A gust of wind blew from behind whipping leaves around and blowing my hair in front of my face. Closing my eyes for a second, I continued walking, my arm firmly linked with Luke's when suddenly my other arm was roughly grabbed. My eyes flicked open but I still couldn't see through the mass of hair flapping and blocking my vision.

"Oy!" I heard Luke yell and his grip on my left arm tightened. I was being pulled in both directions like a rag doll being fought over by two really determined kids. The one on my right was winning, his fingers digging roughly into my skin. Luke pulled back strongly but I could feel his hands slipping. I wished the wind would drop so I could see what was happening, I mean, this was broad daylight in the middle of Rotherham. Who was doing this? One of the hands let go of my right arm and hope surged. Maybe they were giving up. The wind dropped at the same moment and my hair settled down in time for me to see a fat fist fly past my face. I heard a sickening 'thwack' and knew my Luke had been hit, hard.

"Luke!" I cried as his grip vanished. The hand that'd just hurt Luke slammed around my waist and my feet nearly left the floor as I was dragged backwards. Struggling, I saw Luke fall back, his head crashing against the pavement. Blood ran from his lip as his eyes closed. "Luke!"

Digging my nails into the man's arms I writhed and kicked but it did me no good, he was too strong. My feet were no longer on the ground as he flung me backwards and I landed on a cold hard surface. For a second I saw my assailant's face, fat and red with exertion, his eyes and lips narrow and mean.

"Keep quiet in there or you'll regret it!" his deep voice growled as the door slid across and I was left in darkness.

Realising I was inside the white van, for a moment I was too stunned to move. Luke was hurt, I'd been kidnapped. I felt the van tilt as the man lifted his bulk into the driver's seat. The engine fired and I sprang into life. I couldn't let him drive away with me.

"Let me out!" I cried hammering on what I hoped was the door. I felt around for a handle, but there was nothing, the inside was totally flat. I could feel cracks where the door ended and the sides of the van began, but there was nothing to help me open it.

Loud rock music thundered from the cabin. He must've been deafened by it but I knew what he was doing, he was drowning out my cries.

"Help!" I screamed louder, hammering with both fists. "I've been kidnapped!"

Suddenly the van tipped to the right as it cornered sharply and I was thrown first forwards then backwards onto the floor. I struggled to my knees then returned to the edge, frantically pounding on the cold metal. My heart felt like it was gonna burst with fear. Rivers of ice ran up and down my spine, piercing my brain and spinning around in my stomach until I felt sure I'd be sick.

"Help me!" My throat seared with pain, my fists burning but I didn't stop. I had to make somebody hear me.

Suddenly I was thrown sideways as the van stopped.

The door, I must open the door.

Still on my knees my hands groped in the dark, desperate to find a way out. I tipped again as the van started up, swinging first to the left then the right. It must have been a roundabout.

I tried to figure out where we were headed but my brain cells were frozen.

The van picked up speed and there were less twists and turns. He was obviously heading onto faster roads where there'd be less chance of anybody hearing me.

Hot tears pricked my eyes and my throat tightened.

"Let me out." There was no more strength in my voice. I knew no one would hear me. Feeling totally drained, I sank onto the floor. My aching fists tapped but there was no energy in them now, I knew it was hopeless but I couldn't give in completely. Images of Mum, Dad, Gran and my poor hurt Luke swam before my eyes. My bottom lip crumpled and I sobbed, wondering whether I'd ever see any of them again.

***

CHAPTER NINE

I thought about my promise to keep in touch with Gran and Sam. I'd been doing so well since my return from holiday. But now my promise would be broken. There'd be no more contact from me.

Contact. My mobile! I reached around for my bag. It had to be in here somewhere, it'd been over my right arm! Frantically I scrabbled around the floor on my hands and knees feeling in the dark, occasionally being tipped over as the van continued its journey.

"Come on, where are you?" I hissed, swiping away my tears. My eyes had adjusted a little to the dark and I searched for a darker shape, wishing I used a bigger bag. The one I'd picked out today barely held my mobile, a tissue and a few coins.

Several minutes of searching confirmed my worst fears, the bag wasn't there. The man up front must have ripped it from my arm as he thrust me into the van. I pictured it on the pavement, abandoned beside my stricken boyfriend.

"I hope you're all right, Luke," I whispered. "I love you."

I gave up all hope of trying to break out or getting anybody to hear me. It was hopeless. All I could do was wait until he stopped and opened the doors, then maybe, once I'd seen the surroundings, I could work something out. My knowledge of this area was so poor and he'd taken so many twists and turns, I'd no idea where we were. I just hoped he didn't kill me as soon as the van door opened.

Shuffling across to the far side, I pulled my knees up and wrapped my arms around them. I was totally at his mercy, if he had any. Rocking and biting my lip, I'd never felt so alone.

"Mum, Dad, I wish you were here."

There was only one thing that had a little brightness in it. Maybe he was the same man who'd taken Rebecca and maybe he was taking me to her. I shivered. I just hoped he was taking me to a live sister and not a grave.

The journey seemed never ending as my thoughts grew darker and darker. I felt like I'd go totally off my head if the van didn't stop soon. But then what?

The van slowed and this time instead of picking up speed again, it swerved sharply to the right then stopped.

My heart sped up, this was it; we'd arrived. Instantly I wished the journey hadn't ended. While we were moving, as horrible as it was, I was still alive. But surely he hadn't brought me all this way to kill me? My knuckles were almost numb as they gripped my knees.

I felt the van lurch as the driver climbed out and sat, huddled, staring across at the door, waiting for it to slide open. Hearing his footsteps tap around the side, I held my breath, my whole body rigid.

Light blazed in as the door slid noisily back. I closed my burning eyes tight, squinting through tiny slits. His bulk stood silhouetted in the doorway.

"Out, now!" His voice was gruff and loud. Wherever we were he wasn't bothered about anybody hearing him.

I didn't want to move, but was too scared to disobey him, so I shuffled cautiously forwards. As soon as I was within reach he grabbed my arm, wrenching me from the van.

Blinking, I tried to take in my surroundings. We were on an eerily quiet street. Terraced houses lined the road but something wasn't right. As my eyes adjusted I realised what it was. Heavy metal boards covered every door and window. The place was deserted.

The van door slammed shut behind us as he dragged me towards a narrow alley running between the houses. I didn't bother calling out, it was obvious there was no point. There was absolutely nobody to hear me. His grip on my arm felt like rottweilers' teeth, there was no chance of me breaking free. My feet caught on bottles, carrier bags bulging with foul smelling waste and even needles as he pulled me onwards.

Another alley ran along the back of the houses and the man dragged me about half way along before stopping in front of a dilapidated gate. Strips of blue paint had peeled away revealing slats of rotten, broken wood beneath. Its hinges creaked as the man pushed it open and pulled me through.

My whole body trembled as we headed across an overgrown garden towards the house.

"No!" I cried. Planting my feet I tried to pull back but his fingers bit harder into my arm until I cringed with pain. A strong tug broke my foot hold and I stumbled forward into the metal covering on the door.

The man bent the chubby fingers of his free hand around the metal cover, prising it back. It opened

97

from the bottom, just wide enough for him to slide his bulk in to hold it back. The original inside door was fastened with a new, sturdy padlock. My throat closed up so tight I could barely breathe as he slipped his hand into his jacket pocket and retrieved a key.

Pushing me up against the cobwebby brick wall his shoulder pressed hard into my back, pinning me in place while he used both hands to unfasten the lock.

I wanted to scream, to run, to gauge his eyes out, but I couldn't move. I tried to wriggle free, but he only leaned harder until the bricks grazed my face. I decided that as soon as the door swung open and the pressure eased from my back I'd turn and let my finger nails loose on his face.

Pressed into the wall, I couldn't see much but I heard the door squeak as it opened. I tensed, preparing for my chance to escape. But he'd thought of everything. Before he released the pressure from my back his hand clamped onto my right arm. Wincing, I knew I still had to try to escape and as soon as he stepped back, I spun around, my left hand clawing wildly.

"Let me go!" I screamed, gauging my nails down his face.

"Aargh!" he cried, "Why you…!"

Instead of loosening his grip, he tightened it, twisting my arm up my back.

"Help me! Somebody help me!" I screamed.

As I yelled, he pushed me forwards through the gap and I heard the metal shutter snap shut behind us.

Every nerve in my body sparked like electricity. I was trapped.

"Let me go, please!" I begged.

Tiny sunbeams shone through minute holes in the shutters producing a dappled effect on the walls and floor. The whole place looked like it had chicken pox, but the dim light allowed me to make out stained wallpaper with black shapes where pictures once hung and soiled carpets lining the floor. I could hear a drip from somewhere and the whole place smelt of damp.

"Upstairs!" he barked.

"No!" I yelled, struggling. I knew it was no good but I couldn't just let him take me up there. I pulled and twisted but his grip on my arm was so secure it felt like my shoulder would snap out of its socket.

"Rachel!"

I think my heart actually stopped. A girl's voice, one I knew so well, came from upstairs.

"Rebecca?" I called back.

"Yeah. It's okay."

She was telling me to stop fighting. It didn't seem sensible but I trusted her. She was my twin and she was alive. I let my kidnapper push me up the stairs and to the left into what was once a double bedroom.

Rebecca sat on the dusty wooden floor leaning back against the far wall. A long metal chain ran from her right ankle to a ring fastened firmly to the wall behind her. She was dirty and thin, but she was alive.

"What have you done to her, you b …?" Sorry to say, right at that moment I hated him and couldn't stop spewing out a stream of curse words. The sight of my twin sitting chained in this dismal, dirty place was too much.

I pulled forwards, wanting to run to her but he held me back, walking me towards her right.

"Rachel, I'm okay." I swear there was actually a hint of laughter in her voice. I guess she'd never heard me swear before.

I stopped shouting and struggling and that's when I saw it, another ring, about a metre from hers.

An identical chain hung from it, waiting for me. Pushing me down beside Rebecca I noticed for the first time the hammer in his free hand. He must have picked it up somewhere in the room downstairs. Opening a metal loop, he fastened it around my right ankle. This was my last chance to run, but I didn't. I couldn't leave Rebecca behind. I just hoped we could figure out a way to escape once he'd gone.

"Not happy with just one of us, eh? Scumbag!" Rebecca snarled. "Why'd you need us both? Hey? You pervert! You're mental, a head case! Back in the slammer, that's where you're going!"

Her voice was interrupted by the metallic clang of some sort of pin being hammered into my ankle brace. Finally he wiggled it so it bit into my flesh, then he grinned.

"Shout all you want, 'Gob on legs', but I've got you now. You're mine, both of you. I decide whether you get fed or go hungry. I decide whether you live or die. So be nice. Your life depends on it."

Then with a sneer he turned and walked out the door. My blood felt like ice water running through my veins as his footsteps retreated down the stairs. I wanted to run after him, tell him to come back and let us go, but I just sat there. Fear kept the longing in my head and stopped it reaching my legs. I heard the squeak of the back door followed by the metal cover clanging shut, then nothing.

The ensuing silence felt like a death sentence until Rebecca spoke.

"Nice ankle bracelet, hey?"

***

CHAPTER TEN

"Rebecca!" The chain clinked as I twisted around and threw my arms around my twin's neck. "I thought you were dead!"

"Yeah, well, I'm still here. Pschh!" She sucked in air as I squeezed tighter.

"Rebecca?" I let go and sat back staring at my sister through the gloom. "What's wrong?"

"I fought back." A little sarcastic smile crossed her lips. "He didn't like it."

"That's why you warned me?"

Rebecca nodded.

"What hurts?"

"My ribs mostly. I think he might've busted one, or maybe it's just bruised. I don't know."

I looked more closely.

"You've got a black eye."

"Yeah, well that could've happened at the same time, he knocked me out while he put the chain on so I wouldn't escape."

"What?" I gasped. "You could have concussion or anything!"

This was bad, she needed the hospital. Rebecca shook her head.

"No, I'm fine. I didn't feel sick or anything after and once the headache went away I've been okay."

I wasn't totally convinced but I wasn't exactly in a position to do anything about it. I sat for a minute then frowned.

"You said it *could* have happened when you were knocked out. When else could it have happened?"

"Well it might have been the other day. I told him what I thought of him. He didn't like that either." She grinned. "I never could keep my mouth shut."

"Becs, you've got to be more careful, he's dangerous!"

"Yeah, well, I think I've figured that one out."

Her sarcasm was still intact at least.

"Have you been here all the time?"

Rebecca nodded. "Yeah, six days."

Even in this dim light, I could see she wasn't herself. She was still spouting off verbally but it was a front. Her slumped posture was more than just painful ribs. My sister was worried, scared even. There was something in her face that reminded me of Gran after she'd been mugged. My gran had given up.

"How did he get you?"

"A white van stopped beside me on the way to the bus station last Monday. The driver opened the door and asked for directions. As soon as I was close enough he grabbed my arm. At first I was so stunned I didn't do anything. He climbed out of the van still holding me and that's when I kicked off. I shouted for him to let me go but he immediately clamped his sweaty hand over my mouth. So I started to kick. But when I did, he just wrapped his arm around my waist and pulled me tight against him. That was gross he's so fat and stinks of B.O. I tried to look around, I mean, it

102

wasn't that late. I couldn't believe no one could see what was going on. He pushed me up against the side of the van leaning on me so he could let go of my waist and open the door. I tried wriggling free but his great bulk just held me there, I'd got no chance. I tried biting his fingers, but his grip was so hard I couldn't even open my mouth. He pushed me inside the van then slammed it shut. My heart was pumping so hard it actually hurt. I started hammering on the sides straight away and tried opening the door but it was no good. Do you know he's so huge the van rocked when he got back in?"

"Yeah, I know," I said, actually managing a little laugh. "That happened to me. It was like King Kong had climbed in it tipped that much."

Rebecca smiled, "I know, like seriously, lose some weight man!"

We both laughed. It was hard to believe we could in the circumstances but I guess we needed to make fun of him, to somehow make him not so frightening.

"Did he bring you straight here?"

"Yeah." Rebecca looked down at her feet. "I was absolutely petrified when he brought me to this deserted place then started pushing me up stairs. My mind went crazy imagining all sorts of things and that's when I went wild. I kicked, screamed, punched, scratched, you name it. Even when he'd hurt my rib I still didn't stop. I guess that's why he knocked me out."

I looked at my twin remembering how frightened I was until she called to me. For her there was no voice of reassurance.

"I don't know how you coped."

Rebecca shrugged. "Had to. You would have too."

I shook my head. "I don't think so." Looking up at the ceiling, I stared at the bare light bulb and the web of cracks across the artex. "I thought I was gonna die," I said, my voice a whisper. "But not straight away." I stopped, unable to put into words what I'd feared. "When I heard your voice, I was so relieved." Tears pricked my eyes. "I'm so glad you're alive, Rebecca."

"Not more than I am." I could hear the smile in her voice.

"So what's happened since he brought you here? He hasn't done anything … has he?"

"No way!" Rebecca snapped.

"Sorry." I paused. "Do you want to talk about it?"

Rebecca sighed. "There's not much to say. The chain was already here waiting for me. It's totally solid. I've spent the last six days trying to get out of it and all I've got to show for my efforts is a bloody ankle. I feel like the ghost of freaking Marley. When I came round after he'd knocked me out it was pitch black and my ribs and head were killing me. First I was scared he was still here, then more scared that he'd never come back. I thought he'd left me here to starve to death." She was quiet for a minute. I couldn't imagine how terrified she must have been. I wanted to put my arms around her but didn't want to hurt her again.

"I screamed like crazy for the first two days but nobody heard. Every day I hear the roar of trucks, bulldozers, whatever they are, but they're too far away and they make enough noise of their own anyway. I

104

guess they're gradually tearing down this whole freaking estate, but they're not near us yet."

"What about the toilet?"

"The bathroom works." She nodded towards her left. "The chain reaches just far enough to get to the toilet and sink. He must have figured a way to get the water switched on because I can't imagine them leaving it connected when they're knocking the place down. There's no electricity though. It gets dark real early then there's nothing to see or do for hours. I've been going off my head. The jerk only comes long enough to drop food off then goes again. Not that I'd want his company!"

She drew her legs up, wrapped her arms around them then smiled. "It'll be better now you're here. Not that I'd wished for you to be here or anything, but at least now I've got someone to talk to."

"I come in handy sometimes." I returned her smile glad that my being there had helped her. But I couldn't help wishing I was somewhere else, anywhere would do. Even the doctor's or the dentist's would be way better than this.

"So, how did he get you?"

I told her the events of the morning then about seeing her on the news, doing the reconstruction and meeting her parents.

She asked loads of questions about her family wanting to know whether they were okay.

"When did you say you did that reconstruction?" she asked at last.

"I did it on Wednesday and it went on the news on Thursday."

Rebecca frowned. "So *that's* why he figured he'd got the wrong one." She nodded at the wall. "He put that one in on Friday."

Rebecca's words were like spikes sticking into my heart.

"What? You mean he was really after me?"

Rebecca grimaced, like she hadn't meant for me to know.

"Well, it's just that, he came in with this whopping great chain and started hammering the wall. I asked him what he was doing but he just ignored me. 'Hey!' I said and gave him a great kick in the ribs. That got his attention." She paused. "I've never seen anybody so furious. He spun around faster than anybody that size has a right to and grabbed my jumper, pulling it tight at the neck. I could barely breathe. He still had the hammer in his other hand and held it up above my head. I thought *'this is it, I'm gonna die'*, but instead, he threw the hammer down, growling then whacked me across my face. It was so hard I thought all my teeth were going to fall out. And that's when he told me. He knew where one of us was but it turned out he'd actually picked the wrong one up. 'How lucky was that?' he goes. 'Now I can get you both'."

"So he knows we're twins?"

"Well he should."

"Why?"

"Haven't you figured it out yet?"

"No?" I mean, what was I missing here?

"Rach, you're so thick sometimes. The great oaf's our freaking birth dad!"

***

106

CHAPTER ELEVEN

"Our birth dad? The one who wanted to batter us to death when we were babies?"

"The one and the same."

"How do you know?"

"Well, the first few days he just threw food at me and went straight out ignoring all my questions. I reckon he got pleasure out of leaving me guessing. But when I had a right go at him, he ranted on about how he never wanted us and it was our fault Marcy left him."

"So what does he want us for now? He hates us."

"Well, this isn't exactly something you do to somebody you love, is it?"

She'd got a point.

"But why keep us here? Why not, you know, just get rid of us?"

"Well, do you remember, back in the summer when birth brother Mark attacked us? He said his dad wanted Marcy back."

"Yeah?"

"Well, looks like birth dad's figured out Marcy won't want anything to do with a crazy like him. So he's decided to get himself a couple of bargaining chips. Us."

"What? I don't get it. What have we got to do with him and Marcy getting back together?"

"Because he knows how much she wanted us..."

"Oh, you admit that now?" I jumped in.

Rebecca gave me a withering look. "Do you want me to tell you or not?"

"All right, all right. Look, after the day I've had I'm not exactly firing on all cylinders."

"Sorry, Rach. I'm not the calmest person around here right now either."

"Well given there's only the two of us, I reckon you probably are."

Rebecca grinned. "Yeah, I guess. Anyway, I reckon he'll tell her he's got us and if she wants us to stay alive she's got to go back to him."

"But how's that work? I mean. Even if she goes back to him, once he lets us go, she'll leave him."

Rebecca just looked at me.

I slumped back against the wall. If that was really his plan, he'd never let us go. He wouldn't be able to. My throat tightened up so much I couldn't actually speak for a few minutes.

"But that's crazy!" I managed, at last.

"Well this isn't exactly the work of a sane man, is it?"

As I shook my head, my stomach rumbled. I couldn't believe it, all this tension and my stomach still reminded me I was hungry.

"Here, have a sweaty sandwich," Rebecca said, holding out a thin wedge of white bread that flopped in her hands.

"Er, no, that's all right. You must be hungrier than me."

She was so thin, there was no way I could take food off her, not even a manky sandwich.

"Hey, it's okay, it doesn't taste as bad as it looks," Rebecca said, twirling it in her fingers. "It tastes worse, but after a couple of days of hunger you stop being so picky."

I wasn't so sure, not if everything he brought looked like strips of soggy paper. I'd always thought I needed to lose weight but planned to do it with diet and exercise. Being chained to a wall in a filthy condemned ex-house being force fed scabby bread was not my idea of a good way to shed pounds.

Chewing my lip I stared at the far wall. We'd normally be eating our Sunday dinner about this time. Mum, Dad and Luke must be absolutely frantic. I just hoped Luke was okay and had put the police on the right trail with a description of the kidnapper and the white van. When Rebecca was taken there were no clues, but with Luke as a witness they just *had* to find us.

***

"So, is there no way to move this board?" After three hours I was stir crazy. I'd paced the small room four times, investigated the sparse bathroom and now stood in front of the metal board on the window. Fragments of glass crunched beneath my feet.

"Well there wasn't on my own." Rebecca came to join me her chain clanking. "I tried the first couple of days. As you can see, I broke the window to get to it. Bad idea actually, I've been freezing ever since. It's amazing how much cold air comes through those tiny holes."

"What if we try together?" I looked at her hopefully. Rebecca shrugged.

"Might as well give it a go, I've nothing better to do."

We stood side by side our hands on the cold, hard surface.

"After three?"

Rebecca nodded.

"One, two, three!"

Groaning with the effort we pushed as hard as we could. My trainers constantly slipped on the broken glass but I wouldn't give up. The metal board creaked and flexed but held firm.

After several minutes, Rebecca stepped back, holding her ribs.

"It's no good," she said and turned back to her place on the floor.

"Oh, come on, Rebecca, give it another go."

"It's hopeless, Rach. Don't you get it? I know there are two of us now, but we've tried and failed, okay? It's not going to happen."

"So that's it? We just give up?"

"I haven't given up. I'm just being realistic." Rebecca's voice was flat as she slid back down to the floor.

Despair leapt up, grabbing my throat. I'd never seen Rebecca like this. She was the fighter, the one who couldn't be beaten, the one who always bit back. All this time, sitting here alone had changed her, defeated her. I walked over and knelt beside her.

"Becs, please don't give up. I know you've probably tried everything, but, you never know, I might think of something you haven't. Or there might be something you couldn't do on your own but together we could succeed."

Rebecca sighed. "Rach, if you can come up with something good, I'm all ears."

"Right." I scanned around keen not to lose this little spark. "What we need is something to lever that board."

A quick glance was enough to see there was nothing in the bedroom, so I headed into the bathroom. A once white bathroom suite and two manky green radiators were the only contents. The tide-marked bath ran along the left wall. A tiny sink and stained seatless toilet stood in front of me and a boarded up window split the right wall.

"Great, loads of options here," I muttered. "Does the bath work?" I called over my shoulder.

"No," Rebecca replied. "He's only connected up the sink and toilet."

Stepping forwards I examined the bath taps. They were thickly coated in lime scale and looked ancient. I gripped the nearest with both hands and pulled, hard, but it wouldn't budge. The other was no better.

"What about a floor board?" I asked, willing to try anything. "Could we lever one of those up and use it?"

I heard the clank of Rebecca's chain as she came to look.

She shrugged. "We can give it a go, but pull one up from under this lino so Daddy Poos won't notice."

Dropping to my knees, I dug my fingers beneath the edge of the lino beside the bath.

"Ow!" Searing pain shot beneath my finger nails. Wrenching my stinging hands out I quickly scraped pieces of rotten wood from under my nails. "Better watch out for the splinters," I warned.

More warily I tried again, this time trying to keep my fingers from scraping the wood. Rebecca did the same and within seconds a tearing sound accompanied the lino ripping from its securing nails.

"So far, so good," Rebecca said as we rolled the lino back beneath us.

The floor boards ran at 90 degrees to the bath and were rotten near it but solid nearer the outer wall.

"I reckon we should start with the rotten bit, that's gonna come up easiest."

Rebecca nodded.

The boards were fitted close together so we used the chains to rub away the soft wood. It took ages before there was a gap big enough at each side to get our fingers in.

"Okay, after three," I instructed. "One, two, three!"

We both pulled. The floor board creaked and bent.

"It's coming!" This was fantastic, our first breakthrough! We carried on tugging until, with a sharp crack, the plank snapped. With the sudden release of tension we both fell back like skittles, each clutching a small piece of damp timber. I landed on some coiled links of chain and yelped as pain shot through my bottom and up my back.

Dropping the wood, I clutched my coccyx. "Aargh! That hurt, so bad!"

At the sound of giggling I turned and glared at Rebecca.

"The look on your face when it gave way!" she said, still lying where she'd fallen. "I wish I'd got a camera!"

"It hurts!" I said, again, "And it's not funny." But at the same time, a laugh escaped. "I'm gonna have such a bruise!"

"Yeah, well don't ask me to have a look at it for you."

"You're my twin. You should be willing to do anything for me."

"Get real! No way am I looking at your rear end! I might have been kidnapped and locked up in a room for nearly a week but I'm not that far gone!"

"Well, that's a matter of opinion." I grinned and soon we were both laughing.

When we finally settled down we had another go at the floorboard but it was no good. It wouldn't move.

***

Darkness gradually dropped outside turning our room into a black tomb. There wasn't even a chink of light. We were in the back of the house so even if there were any street lights working they'd never reach us.

"What time does he normally bring food?" I asked, settling back in the bedroom and hugging my knees to keep warm. In the last half hour the temperature had really dropped.

"No idea," Rebecca answered. "It's always pitch black so I can't see the time. I think it varies though."

As if in answer my nerves suddenly twitched, alert to the sound of shuffling outside. Seconds later the lock rattled and the door opened downstairs. Reaching out I clutched Rebecca's hand. As desperate as I was for food, I was equally terrified about seeing him again. As his feet advanced, tapping on each stair, I felt my whole body stiffen. By the time he stepped into the room and shone a torch beam directly into my eyes I was rigid with fear. Blinking, I raised my arm to shield myself from the glare.

"Still here then, little rabbits?" he said, in his gruff voice. "Enjoying your nice little home?"

"Shut up, you pervert," Rebecca snarled. "You're pathetic! You can't even get a woman to stay with you without kidnapping her kids and holding them to ransom!"

My chest tightened. *Shut up, Rebecca, just shut up,* my mind urged. Why couldn't Rebecca just keep quiet for once?

Growling, he strode across the room. The light was almost in my face, blinding me, when I felt a waft of cold air and heard a loud slap beside me.

I heard Rebecca gasp, then snap. "Yeah, real brave. Hit a girl who's tied up. Big man, hey?"

"Yeah, real big!" he snarled. "And holding all the cards, including the food. You think you've got it all figured out?" he laughed. "You haven't a clue. I've got plans for you!"

I heard the rustle of plastic, followed by a thud and "Oomph." from Rebecca.

"You'd better make it last. I won't be back tomorrow and next time you mouth off it'll be a week." I felt his hot breath on my cheek and shrank back against the wall, cringing. "You'd better talk to that sister of yours or you'll both starve to death." He laughed as his footsteps receded back across the room. "Think you're smart? You'll soon learn who's in charge!" He was still laughing as his shoes plodded downstairs. The lock clicked outside and he was gone.

"Rebecca, why do you do it?" I said, twisting around. I couldn't see her but it still felt better to face her. "You only make things worse."

Rebecca didn't reply.

"Becs?" My throat tightened in panic. What if he'd knocked her unconscious? How would I help her when I couldn't even see her? "Are you okay?"

"I'm all right," her voice was soft. "Split lip and the wind knocked out of me when he threw the bag into my lap. There's cans in it today and it landed hard on my ribs. Anyway, now it's here, let's see if we can feel our way to a bit of food. We'll have to make it last though. When he says he won't be back tomorrow, he won't."

"He might change his mind."

"Uh, uh. He never has before."

"He's left you without food before?" This was *way* bad.

"You know me and my mouth." There was a little smile in her voice.

I just sank back against the wall, shaking my head. Suddenly having Rebecca here didn't seem such a fantastic idea. With her on my side, I could be in deep trouble.

***

CHAPTER TWELVE

The sandwiches were manky but they were food. I
didn't stop to guess what was in them, they didn't taste
of anything good.

"Probably last week's leftovers," was Rebecca's
opinion.

She only allowed us two each and one of the
cans of cola. At least that's what I think it was. I made
it last for hours and when I set it down my stomach
growled in protest, probably as much with disgust as
hunger.

"Rebecca?"

"Yeah?"

"What do you think he meant when he said 'I've
got plans for you'?"

"Who knows? He was probably just winding us
up."

"But, what if he wasn't? What if there's more
to it than him just getting Marcy back?"

"What if there is? It doesn't alter our situation.
We're still chained to this stupid wall, aren't we?"

"I suppose." I knew she'd got a point but I
couldn't help my worry level going up another notch.
Jed the jerk was way too sure of himself when he said

it. He was planning something and I wasn't sure whether I wanted to know what it was or not.

"Look, we'd better get some sleep. It's been dark for hours," Rebecca suggested. I heard her shuffling down beside me and shivered. "And I think we'd be warmer if we snuggled up together."

I so was cold I definitely wasn't gonna argue with that one! I lay down on the bare wooden boards and inched forwards until my front was against Rebecca's back. We huddled as closely as we could. It felt weird, I was only just getting to know Rebecca and here I was snuggling up to her. I put the thought out of my mind, survival was all that mattered.

Even though we were close my back was still exposed. Cold drafts wafted around me and although I was totally exhausted it seemed like hours before I finally managed to nod off. I lay there envious as Rebecca's breathing quickly became steady and I was left listening to the annoying drip, drip of the cold water tap in the bathroom, wondering whether we'd ever get out of there.

***

"That's the best night's sleep I've had since I've been here," Rebecca announced the next morning.

The room was back to its usual day time dimness but my eyes were used to it now and once I'd rubbed the sleep out, I could see clearly enough.

"It was my worst," I muttered, yawning.

Rebecca shrugged. "Well it's not exactly the Ritz, but you'll get used to it eventually. I didn't sleep at all for the first three nights. By then I was so totally exhausted I fell asleep straight away but the cold kept waking me up. Having you behind me last night kept me so much warmer. I didn't wake up once."

"I noticed. Your heavy breathing made me jealous."

"Well, I'll tell you what. I'll snuggle up to your back tonight, see if that helps."

"Thanks."

I couldn't exactly sound very enthusiastic. The thought of even one more night in that derelict house was totally depressing.

Monday was my worst day at school with seriously boring lessons, but given the choice between that and the dim room I'd have swapped in a second.

In the distance the sound of heavy machinery started up.

"Is that the workmen?" Standing, I hurried over to the shutter. "Do you think they'll hear if we both shout?"

Rebecca shook her head. "No, they're too far away. Maybe when they get closer?"

I sagged like an unsupported puppet and dragged myself back over to Rebecca.

"It's hopeless, isn't it?" I said, flopping down beside her.

"No, we just have to be patient."

"For how long?"

Rebecca shrugged. "How about a game of 'I spy'?"

"Yeah, sure, Becs. I spy with my little eye something beginning with W."

"Walls."

"Yep, game over." I didn't want to be mean but everything seemed so hopeless I felt like I'd go out of my mind if I had to stay there much longer.

"Oh, Rach. Where's your imagination? Come on, I've just spent days occupying myself. It's got to be doubly better now you're here." She dug her elbow into my ribs. "Come on. I spy with my little eye, something beginning with S."

I felt bad for her and real selfish for being so miserable after only one day, but I couldn't help it. There wasn't a 'Polly Anna' bone in my whole body. If this last year had taught me anything, I now knew that I was a cup half empty person whereas Rebecca was a cup half full. When we were born she must have got all the positive genes and me all the negative.

"Well it can't be shadows 'cause it's too dark," I muttered.

"Nope, it's not shadows." Rebecca was sounding way more cheerful than the situation deserved.

"Shoes."

"No."

"Sad twins."

Rebecca chuckled. "Nope."

I looked around the empty room.

"I haven't got a clue. I give up."

"Spider!" she said, triumphantly.

"Where?" I asked, peering into the gloom.

"About to climb on your shoulder."

"Aargh!" I jumped up like I'd been prodded with a spike, my chains rattling in protest. "Where? It's not on me is it?" Dancing around, I frantically brushed my shoulders.

Rebecca drew up her legs, laughing.

"Rebecca! Shut up and tell me where the spider is!"

Barely able to talk for laughing, she pointed high up on the wall behind me.

I turned around and could just make out a small spider in the far corner of the room.

"But that's no where near me!" I protested.

"Yeah, but you should've seen your face and talk about move! It's like you'd sat on nettles!" Wrapping her arms around her middle she groaned. "Oh, my ribs! That was *so* funny!"

I clenched my fists, as if this situation wasn't bad enough, where'd she get off making fun of me? I opened my mouth to tell her exactly what I thought of her little joke then stopped. My painfully thin twin, who I'd thought lost, was rolling around on the dusty floor of our prison, laughing like the world was okay.

My anger melted like cheese on a toasty and I managed a smile.

"You're an idiot!" I said. "You totally freaked me out."

"I know!" She grinned. "It was priceless."

Shaking my head, I dropped down beside her.

"I'm gonna be insane by the time we get out of here!" I said then wished I hadn't. The atmosphere instantly changed, neither of us wanting to say what passed through our minds. What if we never did get out of there?

***

CHAPTER THIRTEEN

At one o'clock we allowed ourselves two sandwiches each and another can of pop, then tried to occupy ourselves for the afternoon.

No matter how much imagination anybody had there was no way to keep busy all those empty hours. Tired after little sleep, I drifted off here and there but the day still dragged. I was actually glad when it got dark and we lie down for the night. Rebecca snuggled up to my back as promised and it did make me feel warmer. Falling asleep quickly, I actually slept through and woke with a totally dead right arm the next morning. Painfully stretching, I found Rebecca already sitting up, awake.

"Couldn't you sleep?" I asked.

She shook her head. "I was alright for the first half of the night but my stomach was aching too much after that."

"Is it your time of the month?"

She shook her head. "No, I'm just hungry, I think."

"Or maybe it's these grotty sandwiches. Mine definitely tasted suspect yesterday."

Rebecca smiled, but it was sad and tired. "Yeah, he's not exactly Jamie Oliver, is he?"

I shook my head. "How many sandwiches have we got left?"

Rebecca opened the plastic bag and peered inside.

"Seven," she counted.

"Right, well you have two now. I'll have one. Then we've both got two for lunch time. When the jerk comes back later we'll be restocked."

"I never eat everything," Rebecca said. "Just in case he doesn't come when he says he will."

"Has he done that before?" My chest tightened.

"No, I just like to be careful."

"But, what if he has an accident or something?" I pictured the white van sandwiched between two trucks on a motorway pileup.

"Look, we can't worry about stuff like that, we'd go mental. Let's just save a couple of sandwiches and hope he turns up. Okay?"

"Okay," I said, but found it impossible to get the image from my mind.

"We'll have one each for now, okay?" Rebecca said as the rumbling of distant machinery started up

"Okay," I agreed. My stomach felt real empty but Rebecca was so thin from managing on rubbish rations like, forever, it made me feel guilty eating anything at all.

"Do you think they're looking for us?" I asked, quietly.

"Well, duh! Of course they're looking," Rebecca said, sticking her hand into the sandwich bag. "Now, let me see," she murmured. "Totally rank cheese or limp lettuce? Limp lettuce has it. Nothing to beat limp lettuce when a girl's starving."

"No, I mean, they might know about the white van now but I doubt Luke got the registration number and I bet they don't even know the jerk's out of prison. Add to that the fact we're in the middle of an estate that's being demolished, like, how are they gonna find us? How would they even know where to start looking?"

"That's right, put a girl right off her breakfast," Rebecca muttered, lowering her hand, her lettuce sandwich flopping like a dog's tongue. Probably tasted like it as well.

"Don't stop eating," I said quickly, wishing I'd kept my big mouth shut. "You need it."

Rebecca sighed and took another bite.

"Polith have their wayth," she said with her mouth full.

"Yeah, sure they do," I said. *But they aren't miracle workers.*

***

As evening fell and the room gave itself over to darkness, I sat with my legs drawn up. Chewing my thumb nail I waited for the sound of the lock rattling open. It was such a weird feeling. I hated the man and never wanted to see him again, but he was our only source of food, so another part of me waited like a four-year-old desperate to see Father Christmas.

"When will he come?" I asked for about the tenth time.

"Like I said every time you asked before. I don't know," Rebecca said. "He comes when he wants. We're not exactly his top priority."

"Well we should be!" I snapped. "I mean, he grabbed us off the streets and chained us up in this condemned rat trap. The least he could do is turn up at a regular time with our food!"

Just then the rattle of the lock sounded downstairs and every nerve in my body sparked with a mixture of relief and fear.

"Behave yourself, Rebecca," I hissed. "Don't say anything to rack him off. We need the food."

Rebecca grunted beside me.

"Please!" I pleaded.

Sitting rigid, I listened to his feet advance up the stairs then cringed as his huge body entered the room. My eyes were getting used to the dark and from the glow of his torch I could just make out his leering features as he came towards us.

"Still here then?" he mocked, raising his torch to our faces.

I blinked, bringing my arms up to shield my eyes from the sudden brightness.

"Look's like you must be happy here," he said, "Regular little holiday for you both."

Heat rose in my body, he was actually getting some sadistic pleasure out of keeping us prisoners.

"Well if you're gonna keep us here you could at least give us a blanket each. It's freezing at night," I snapped before my brain connected.

"What do you think this is?" he growled, "A hotel? You bitches want to be grateful I'm bringing you food. I could just leave you here to rot."

"Dead hostages aren't much use though, are they?" I growled back.

He knelt down in front of me, so close I could smell his tobacco breath.

"And how is my beloved wife gonna know whether you're alive or dead? I've only to take a trainer or boot for her to know I've got you, she won't know whether I took it off a corpse, now will she?"

My chest tightened so much it actually hurt as fear oozed around my body.

"And as for your parents, I've only to send them your jackets and they'll hand over a bunch of cash."

"You're holding us for ransom?" So that was his other plan. And if our parents paid up…?

"Don't get your hopes up." I could hear the sneer in his voice. "Paying the ransom doesn't mean they'll get their precious kiddies back. Why would I want to let you go when we're having such a good time together?"

I felt my eyes sting and bit my lip. I wouldn't give him the satisfaction of seeing me cry.

"Leave her alone." Rebecca's voice was cold but firm.

"Leave her alone?" He laughed loud and deep. "Or else what? You'll rattle your chains at me?"

He stood abruptly, aiming a kick first at me then Rebecca. I yelped, twisting my legs away, my left shin throbbing.

"Worthless the two of ya! Never should've been born! You should've died the night I knocked her from pillar to post, but no, not you, you had to go and live. Well, you might've got between my Marcy and me before but not this time. Now you're gonna put it right again, then there'll be no more need for you."

He turned to go, the bag of food still in his hand.

"Our food!" Rebecca yelled as he left the room.

"Our food!" he called back sarcastically. "If you want it, you'd better fetch it."

I heard a thud as he dropped the bag on the stairs and continued down.

"The pig!" Rebecca hissed as his footsteps receded. Scrambling up she dragged her chain across the floor. "Oh, we've no chance!" she yelled.

I heard him laugh as I went to join her.

"It's nearly half way down," I said, my heart falling like autumn leaves. "I'm sorry Becs, I told you not to say anything and then I opened my big mouth. Now we'll starve. We're never gonna get that."

"We're going to have to," Rebecca's voice was determined.

"Oh, yeah, like, how?"

Rebecca looked at me. "You'll have to do it."

"Me? How am I supposed to reach it?"

"I don't know yet, but your chain's fastened further along the wall than mine so you're about a metre closer to it."

I just gave Rebecca a look. I mean, like that little bit of distance was supposed to make the impossible possible.

"Okay, Smart Alec, come up with a suggestion then."

Rebecca frowned. "I'm thinking."

"Well think fast," I said, "Because that bag doesn't look very steady and in a couple of minutes it'll slide even further down."

There was more chuckling from downstairs as the metal shutter opened and closed, the lock clicking into place.

"And good riddance," Rebecca snarled then sighed. "Okay, right. We know you can't reach it standing up the chain just isn't long enough. But if you lie on your stomach and slither down there you might be able to reach it with your hands."

"Slither down? I'm not a freaking snake, you know. What if I slip and my whole weight goes on my

ankle where the chain's attached? It could break."
Staring down at the carrier bag balanced half on and
half off the distant step I knew I had no choice. I had to
try or we'd starve. "You're gonna have to hold my
ankles and take my weight. Okay?"

"Yes ma'am!" Rebecca said with a crisp salute.

Sighing, I lay down, my lower body still in the
room but my upper body protruding over the small
square landing. The stairs were on my right, steep and
covered in a threadbare carpet so dirty its colour was
impossible to detect. The bulky white carrier bag sat
precariously seven steps down. It leaned ominously
over the edge emitting occasional crackles as its
contents shifted. Twisting to the right, I stepped down
on my hands, dragging my body after me. I felt
Rebecca grip my calves as my hands walked further
down. After only three steps my arms were wobbling.

"Keep a good grip," I groaned. "I haven't got
much upper body strength and right now all my
weight's on my hands."

It didn't help that the carpet was really slimy,
layers of dust and damp having coated each step with a
disgusting paste.

I was only two steps away from reaching the
carrier but already only my feet remained on the
landing. Not for the first time I cursed being so short.
My arms strained as more of my weight shifted
forwards.

"I'm gonna fall!" I gasped.

"No, you're not, I've got your legs," Rebecca
reminded me.

"I know. My ankles are killing me! Try not to
grip the bracelet thing."

"I'm trying," Rebecca's voice was strained
now. "But you're heavy and my ribs are killing me."

I finally made it to the step above the carrier. With my tongue sticking out supposedly helping my concentration, I switched all my weight to my left hand.

Okay, this is it, Rachel.

I steadied myself as best I could then reached for the handle.

Everything happened fast. My left arm buckled, unable to support my weight. I slipped forwards, my chest sliding over the top of the bag, trapping it beneath me. Rebecca yelled as the sudden increase in weight dragged her forwards and she landed face down on the stairs with a loud, "Oomph!"

The impact made her let go of my legs and with no support I bumped front first down each step until the chain snapped tight and the ankle bracelet dug into my skin.

"Aargh!" I screamed as all my weight focused on the one ankle. "Get me up Rebecca! Get me up now! My ankle's gonna break!" The bottom half of my leg burned with pain and sent fiery spikes shooting way past my knee. Tears streamed from my eyes as I struggled to push myself back up.

A cascade of cola cans fell from the upended bag, bouncing on each step before finally thudding against the wall at the bottom.

I heard Rebecca groan as she tried to get a good position to pull me up. Finally I felt her grasp my legs just below the knees.

"Grab the bag on your way past," she ordered, her voice strained as she pulled "And use your other arm to help. You're heavy."

Normally I wouldn't let her get away with a comment like that but I was literally in no position to argue.

I don't know how we did it but with a mixture of me pushing and Rebecca pulling I slowly edged back up the stairs, legs first. The dangerous bit came when I slid back over the bag and tried to grab it again. This time I stabilised myself with my stronger right arm and gripped the bag with the left.

"Pull!" I hissed, terrified I'd fall back down again as my right arm wobbled.

"Yeah!" Rebecca groaned.

Somehow I managed to wrap the handle of the bag around my left wrist and continued to use that arm to push myself up. It seemed to take hours but was probably just a few minutes before I reached the landing and collapsed beside Rebecca.

"Never again," I said, my ankle throbbing. Looking down, I could see blood flowing from where the bracelet had cut into my skin and couldn't help more tears forming. "I can't do this, Rebecca. I'm not brave like you. I can't cope with the pain and fear and hunger. I know I'm a wimp but I can't do it. I just want to go home."

Rebecca's arms slipped around my shoulders as the whole of my insides filled with dark despair. I couldn't go on, but I couldn't see a way out. Were we going to die here?

"I'm not brave," she said, softly, "I'm just a good actress. I was terrified I wouldn't have the strength to pull you up. I thought you'd be stuck down there in agony until Jed came back and I'd just have to watch, listening to you cry. I couldn't stand that."

Her voice broke on the last words and her sobs joined mine. I could feel her shoulders heaving and her tears wet my neck as we hugged, right there at the top of those stinking stairs.

"Will we ever get out of here, Becs?" I asked when the crying had eased off enough for me to speak.

Rebecca didn't answer straight away instead she pushed me back so that I was looking straight into her red-rimmed eyes.

"I don't know but we've got to believe there's hope," she said, "If we give up he'll win and there's no way I'm letting him do that. Anyway we have to keep going for our families' sakes. We have to see them again."

My bottom lip trembled. Just thinking about Mum, Dad, Gran and Luke, hurt like crazy.

"We'll get out. Somehow," I managed, trying to believe it.

Rebecca smiled weakly and nodded. "We don't give up. Okay?"

"Okay."

I decided to keep my family's faces in the front of my mind all the time and picture them if ever I felt like giving up again.

"We need to do something about that leg of yours," Rebecca said. "You don't want it to go septic or anything."

Great, something else to worry about.

We struggled up and dragged our chains behind us to the bathroom. I held mine in my hand to stop it pulling on my ankle. The smallest movement of the anklet sent agonies of pain spiraling around it.

"At least it's not broken," I said, grimacing, "But it really hurts when I put my weight on it."

"It might be sprained or just bruised on the inside. You're lucky it's not broken with all your weight suddenly dropping on it like that."

"Will you stop going on about my weight?" I snapped. "I know I'm bigger than you, but I'm not that fat."

"I never said you were."

"Well, you keep bringing it up."

"When?"

"Like on the stairs, when you said I was heavy."

"Yeah, well you were. Anybody over four stone would've been heavy to hold with my busted ribs but I wouldn't call them fat. It's just an expression, Rach, not a criticism."

"Oh." I didn't really know what else to say. Maybe I was a bit over sensitive about my weight. Sam was always saying it was fine, but I thought she was just being a good mate.

"He hasn't given us any first aid stuff and there's no hot water, but I've got this." Rebecca changed the subject and pulled a lighter out of her pocket, flicking it on.

"What're you gonna do with that?" I stared at the flame, my heart fluttering.

Rebecca tutted. "It's okay, I'm not going to burn you with it. I just thought we could put some water in a small container and heat it up somehow. It might at least be more sterile to dip a cloth in and clean your wound."

"You'll never boil water with that."

Rebecca rolled her eyes. "Well, duh! Who said anything about boiling it? Warm water will at least be better than cold."

I wasn't entirely convinced but didn't suppose it'd do any harm. I just had to hope these chains hadn't been anywhere really manky. Rebecca fished around in the bag and found a plastic sandwich container.

"That's a first," she muttered, tipping the sandwiches out into one of the sandwich bags.

She put a centimeter of water into the plastic container then lit the lighter and held it underneath.

"Do you know how long that's gonna take to warm up?" I said, shaking my head. "I'll have died of septicemia before then and what if the plastic melts?"

"Oh, shut up moaning!" Rebecca griped. "If you've got any better ideas, I'm all ears, other than that just start rinsing off some of the excess blood and wipe the surrounding area with toilet paper or something."

Toilet paper, great, real hygienic. Unfortunately Daddy Poos never thought of supplying us with towels or kitchen roll. Probably his way of reminding us we're kidnapped and not in a hotel, as if we could forget. Or maybe he's such a scruff the idea of washing never entered his thick head.

As I lifted my foot to rest it in the sink I realised how bitter my thoughts were becoming, at least towards our birth dad. Was that normal under these circumstances? I mean, how could anyone not be bitter towards somebody who'd kidnapped you, chained you up and made you nearly kill yourself just to get food? Slight exaggeration, well big, actually, but that's how it felt.

I turned on the tap and gasped. The water wasn't only icy cold, it also stung like crazy when it hit the cut. I slid the bracelet or anklet if I'm to be precise, out of the way as carefully as I could and did my best to wash away the excess blood.

"It's still bleeding," I said, my stomach churning.

"We'll have to find something to fasten round it then. Look this is a bit warm, let's have a look at it."

132

Rebecca tore off a handful of toilet paper and dipped it in her warm water before stepping over and peering at my ankle.

"That looks pretty bad," she said before dabbing the tissue on the wound.

It actually felt warmer than I'd expected but I still sucked in air with each touch.

"That kills," I hissed.

"Drama Queen."

"I'm not a Drama Queen. It really hurts!"

"But it's not gonna kill you, is it?"

"Depends on whether it gets infected or not."

Rebecca tutted in answer and kept on dabbing, occasionally tearing off new toilet paper and dabbing it in her rapidly cooling water.

"Take off one of your socks," she said, when she'd dried it with yet more toilet paper.

"Why?"

"We need something to wrap around it to stop the bleeding."

"Not a sock!"

"It's either that or your bra." Rebecca's face was straight, she really wasn't joking.

Out of the two, I figured my bra was the cleanest and the biggest, my socks were tiny, ending just above my heel. Still balancing on one leg, I managed to get both arms behind me and unhooked it. Then I reached first inside my right sleeve, pulling the strap down, then inside the left sleeve and pulled the bra through.

It actually worked out quite well. Because I'm not that little, there was enough material to wrap around a couple of times. Then Rebecca somehow managed to fasten it tight using its own hooks.

"Ow!" I yelped as she gave a final tug and hooked it on.

"Got to be tight to stop the blood," she said.

"That's so tight it'll stop all circulation. My foot's gonna be so starved of blood it'll shrivel and die."

"D.Q," Rebecca muttered.

"I'm NOT a Drama Queen."

"You so are."

"No, I'm not."

Rebecca just looked at me, her eyebrows raised.

"All right, yes I am, but I've not been through anything like this before."

"And I have?"

"You've had six days more experience than me. You're a veteran."

Rebecca shook her head and grinned.

"Yeah, sure."

"Well you have." I was joking now and Rebecca knew it.

"Come on, let's go sit down and see what goodies our benefactor brought us today," she said, gently thumping my arm, then wincing in pain.

"Your ribs hurt a lot?"

"Only when I move or breathe."

"Oh, that's okay then. You'll just have to hold your breath, like, forever."

"Yeah, right. Great idea, Rach."

I hobbled after her.

"Wonder whether it'll be gone off cheese, damp lettuce or some kind of indistinguishable meat," I mused.

"Yep," Rebecca called back over her shoulder. "All of the above."

***

CHAPTER FOURTEEN

"He's late," I muttered, taking a last look at my watch before everything was totally dark. It was day four of my captivity and my ankle was still throbbing after my stair slide the previous evening.

"Told you, he never sticks to the same time," Rebecca said. "So technically, he's not late."

I chewed my lip. Having to rely on somebody else really wound me up especially when that person was a kidnapper who basically hated us. It didn't exactly instill me with loads of confidence and my grumbling stomach didn't help either. But Rebecca had more experience of him than me so I took a few slow breaths and tried to calm down.

"Can we have those last two sandwiches?" I asked.

"No," she said, firmly, "Not until after he's been."

Which basically showed how much confidence she had in him. Like, none.

"But I'm starving!" I wailed, cringing when I realised I sounded like a five-year-old.

"And I'm not?"

"Sorry, Becs. I'll go get a drink of water. Maybe if I fill myself with liquid I won't feel so hungry."

I limped into the bathroom and held an empty mini cola bottle under the cold water tap in the sink. When it was full I gulped it down in one go, then refilled it.

"If he doesn't come soon, I'm gonna spend all night on the toilet," I said, sinking down beside Rebecca. "I've drunk enough to fill a reservoir already.

"Yeah, slight exaggeration there."

I pulled a face but it was totally wasted in the dark.

"I'm gonna have to start doing exercises or something," I groaned, "I'm so stiff I feel like a ninety-year-old. Trouble is, when I'm on my feet, my ankle kills."

"Who's a little moaner today?" Rebecca said laughter in her voice.

"Yeah, well, it's one of my many talents and my teachers always tell me to play to my strengths."

"Well, they got that one wrong."

"Wish you were still on your own?" I teased.

"NO!" Rebecca's answer came fast and sharp. "I never want to be on my own again, ever, anywhere. You can moan all you like, feel free."

Her vehemence shocked me, I hadn't realised just how hard it must have been on her own all that time.

"Don't worry, I'm not going anywhere." I said, rattling my chain for emphasis.

"Good," she murmured then fell into silence.

***

A couple of hours later we knew our birth dad wasn't coming.

"What're we gonna do?" I asked, fear squeezing my stomach as much as hunger.

"We'll just have to save these last two sandwiches until tomorrow and hope he comes then." Rebecca's voice was steady but deeper than normal like she was trying too hard to keep it from cracking. "Maybe he just got held up somewhere."

"Or maybe, he's punishing us because I dissed him yesterday, asking for the blanket and everything."

Rebecca didn't reply. Great, she thought it was my fault as well.

"How long has he gone before without coming?" I asked.

"One day," she answered. "If he doesn't come in the morning, he'll be here by tomorrow night."

***

But the next night came and he didn't. We'd saved our miserable two sandwiches until lunch. They'd tasted rancid by then but were all we had. All our pop had gone and we'd been reduced to water from the bathroom for the last three hours. I thought about the spilt cans lying at the bottom of the stairs totally unreachable and clenched my fists. For all Jed the birth dad knew all our food lay there with them. We could starve for all he cared.

"He's never gone this long before," Rebecca murmured.

"It's my fault, isn't it? He's gonna let us die because of me." My eyes stung. I didn't want to die there, chained up and slowly starving.

"No." Rebecca said, firmly. "Look, he's never left me this long before and I've said worse things to him than you. If he was that mad he'd have hit you. He's done it to me often enough."

137

I peered at my twin through the dark, "Has he hit you more than you've told me already?"

Rebecca paused. "Some."

"You okay?"

"Same as before you knew about it."

I didn't know what to say. I figured going back to the original subject was safest.

"So, what do you think's happened to him?"

Rebecca shook her head. "I don't know, maybe the police picked him up. They could be questioning him now."

"What if he doesn't tell them where we are?"

"What? And face murder charges? I don't think so. If the police have him, he'll try to hold out but in the end he'll tell them so he'll get a lighter sentence."

"But what if it's not soon enough?"

Rebecca looked at me for a minute. "It will be."

Twisting back to the front I voiced my worse fear.

"What if Marcy's gone back to him and he's not bothered about us now? What if he's decided to let us die?"

I sensed Rebecca shaking her head.

"Not yet. If she's just gone back to him she might ask questions. He'd want to keep us alive for a while just in case."

"So where is he then?" I snapped.

Rebecca didn't answer.

"Look, I know you said before not to worry about it but I can't help it. What if he has had an accident? What if he's lying in a hospital bed unconscious or even dead? What happens to us then?"

"Rach, has anybody ever told you, you're a pain?" Rebecca snapped.

I looked at her stunned.

"Don't you think I've thought all those things? But I'm trying to keep them out of my head. Don't you get it? The minute we give in to thoughts like that we're done for! We've got to stay positive and not give up. He's got held up, that's all. He'll be here, okay?"

I didn't believe her. My heart and mind screamed the opposite, but I nodded anyway.

"Okay."

"Look, we've got to get some sleep, conserve our energy. Then tomorrow, we'll try shouting to the workmen. They're closer now. The noise of their equipment is loads louder. If we can start shouting before all the machinery gets switched on, you never know, they might hear us. And if they don't then we try again at the end of the day as soon as they turn their equipment off. Right?"

"Right," I said, miserably. The workmen were definitely nearer but I didn't think they were close enough. Maybe in a couple more days … but without food I wondered whether *we'd* still be here. I tried to remember how long a person can go without food, so long as they've got water, but my brain wouldn't co-operate.

It took me ages to get to sleep that night, what with my stomach rumbling like an earthquake and my mind conjuring up images of skeletons found in demolished houses.

**

The next morning I woke to the sound of machinery. Rubbing my eyes, I sat up and groaned. I looked down at Rebecca still fast asleep beside me.

"Becs," I said, shaking her. "Becs, the workmen are already here."

"Ugh?" Rebecca squinted up at me then groaned. "They got here early."

I glanced at my watch. "No, looks like we slept late. It's nine o'clock."

"Nine? I've never slept that late the whole time I've been here!" She sat up and checked her watch, like she didn't believe me.

"Maybe it's because we're hungry."

"I would've thought that'd keep us awake," she muttered. "Unless we're getting weaker."

"Don't say that!" I snapped. "Come on, let's shout."

Rebecca rolled her eyes, an expression she used a lot with me.

"There's no point now," she said, "There's too much racket out there. Nobody'd hear us. We'll try tonight when they switch everything off."

"But that's another day without food!" I jumped up in desperation and headed to the window, ignoring the pain in my leg. "HELP!" I shouted, banging on the metal grid. "HELP! We're trapped in here! Anybody! Help!"

"You're wasting your time," Rebecca said, flatly.

"Well, it's mine to waste, isn't it? I've nothing better to do around here."

"Hey, don't snap at me. It's not my fault. I'm not the one who went looking up our birth family."

"Oh, so this is all my fault, is it? Well, don't forget, I didn't look up our mother and father. They found me, remember? Marcy'd been spying on my gran for ages before I went to visit her."

"Oh yeah, that's right. It's Marcy's fault. She should've left us alone after dumping us. This is all her fault."

"Don't blame her. She didn't want to leave us. She was trying to save our lives."

"Yeah, sure."

My jaw tensed.

"You've had it in for her from day one, haven't you? The birth dad was the problem, not her. He threatened to kill us, so she did the only thing she could to save us."

"Oh, yeah?" Rebecca was on her feet now and heading towards me. "The only thing? She could have gone to social services and asked for help. She could have gone into a battered wives' home and kept us. She could have left him and gone back to her parents. She could have given us up for adoption. Anything rather than leaving us on a stupid doorstep at a stupid hospital where anybody could've picked us up!"

"She stayed and watched. She made sure a nurse found us and that we were okay. Then, after she'd grassed up the jerk and had him thrown in prison, she came looking for us."

"Too little, too late," Rebecca spat.

"You're never gonna forgive her are you?"

"Not in this life time." Rebecca's voice was sure and final.

"Then it's you who'll hurt. Keeping hold of hate eats you alive. My dad taught me that and he's right."

"Yeah, well I might not be alive very long so it won't really matter, will it?"

With stooped shoulders Rebecca turned from me and walked slowly back to the wall. Dropping into

141

her usual position, she pulled up her knees and rested her head on them, her arms hugging them tight.

The whole of my insides sank like an anchor. Rebecca was the one with hope, she was the one who kept me going. I couldn't go on if she was defeated. Limping over to her, I dropped onto my knees beside her.

"Don't give up, Becs. We're not gonna die. You said so. We've got to think positive. Keep going. We can't give in."

Rebecca's head lifted. "Will you not use my empty encouragements back on me please?"

I smiled and felt my insides lift as Rebecca smiled back.

"So, how about a game of 'I Spy'?" I suggested.

Rebecca rolled her eyes. "Go on then, you first."

***

Our argument was soon forgotten, but the day wasn't. It dragged on like none before. We played every game we could think of, including O's and X's and hangman in the dust. It was such a relief when the dim light dropped even further and the sounds of the machinery gradually stilled one by one. We looked at each other in silent agreement and headed quickly over to the window. As soon as the last engine stopped, we shouted.

"HELP! Help us in here! Help, we're locked in!" Hammering on the metal between shouts, it sounded so loud to us. "HELP!"

Hearing one car after another start up then fade into the distance, we shouted all the louder."

"HELP! HELP US!"

Gradually the silence outside was complete.

"Help!" I tried again, refusing to give up hope. "Help!" I hammered some more before feeling Rebecca's hand on my shoulder.

"It's no good, they're gone."

"They can't be," I said, feeling my eyes burn. "There might be one left, using his mobile or having a smoke or something?" I was so desperate I was ready to wish for anything.

"Rach, it's been fifteen minutes. People don't talk for that long on mobiles and I've never seen a fag yet that could last that long."

All the air in my body escaped in one puff and my shoulders slumped.

"I'm starving, Becs. I'm really starving."

"I know," she said, wrapping her arms around me. "Me too."

***

CHAPTER FIFTEEN

"How many days now without food?" I asked the next morning. A great empty void sat where my stomach should have been.

"Three, well, two if you count the two sandwiches we had left. He last brought food Tuesday night and it's Saturday now." Rebecca's voice was flat, weak.

I knew how she felt. Even pulling myself up to go to the bathroom was a huge effort, one that I did as little as possible.

Our main energy usage was when we shouted and hammered for the workmen to hear us. They were getting nearer now, but our voices and energy levels were dropping at the same rate.

As evening crept in, we sat slumped against the wall, huddled together for warmth.

Suddenly I jumped.

"Did you hear that?" My heart sped up so much it felt like it'd trip over itself.

Rebecca tilted her head.

"It was the lock," she whispered, her grip tightening on my arm.

I hardly dared breathe as I listened. Was it Jed or somebody else? Jed never arrived while there was still an essence of daylight left so this was too early for him. If it was somebody else they might help us and we needed to shout before they gave up and went away. But if it was Jed he'd be real angry if he heard us shouting. And what if it was somebody who'd hurt us? We weren't exactly in a position to defend ourselves. My throat tightened, desperate to make the right choice.

In the end I did nothing, too full of doubts and fear to make any sensible decisions. I sat rigid, listening as the door downstairs creaked open and footsteps sounded on the stairs accompanied by muttering. A male voice. I strained, trying to hear what it was saying and work out whether it was Jed or not. My heart was banging so loud now it felt like my ribs would break.

"… too near, way too near … have to move..." The voice was deep and troubled.

When the footsteps reached the top of the stairs I sucked in air and forgot to let it out again, waiting for the intruder to emerge through the doorway. A bulky figure turned into the room and I finally breathed out as I recognised Jed, the birth dad, jerk. Rebecca's grip on me relaxed.

"Still here then?" he grinned, but there was something in his voice. Was it relief?

"Why'd you leave us so long, you jerk?" Rebecca barked, in an amazingly strong voice given how hungry and weak she was. "We could've died!"

"Shush, Rebecca!" I couldn't believe she was doing this. I could see the carrier bag in his hand, I could smell the food. My mouth was already watering for the sandwiches that just a few days ago I'd found repulsive.

"Listen to your sister, Rebecca," Jed's voice was sarcastic, "Or I might just turn around and take the food right back with me."

Rebecca's intake of breath was so sharp I heard it, but she didn't speak.

"That's better," he said, his grin widening. "It's amazing how a few days without food can teach you who's boss."

He swung the bag backwards and forwards tormenting us with it.

"The police came to see me," he said, his happy expression making me real nervous. "They invited me down to the station to 'help with their enquiries'. Grilled me for hours, they did, but came up with zip. You know why?" He swung the torch up so that it highlighted his own face. The shadows made him look more grotesque than usual and his grin really freaked me out. "Because I'm too smart for 'em. Thought they'd hit pay dirt when they found out I owned a white van. They took it in for forensic testing and everything; but they didn't find a thing 'cause I fooled 'em. When I picked you two hitchhikers up I used another van. It looks just like mine." His laugh, deep and loud made me feel sick. "Seems they don't have a registration number, just a description. The one I used doesn't even belong to a 'known associate'. It belongs to a friend of a friend who's more than happy to stick it to the police. I told 'em, I've been in prison, how am I supposed to know where you are and why would I care? You're nothing to me. Haven't seen you in fourteen years. I said, I'm a good boy, I've got a job now and see my probation officer when I should. Of course, I had to stay away from here for a few days until I got my van back and made sure they weren't following me. So now the police know I had nothing to do with your disappearance they'll leave me alone and look somewhere else." He dropped down onto his haunches in front of us. "Just a pity they'll never find you now."

My arms and fists were rigid. I so wanted to jump up and hit him, to scratch his eyes out, bite and kick him, but I knew I couldn't. We were chained in and even though I hated this man with every cell in my body, he was our only source of food. I couldn't do anything. I just tried to cling to the thought of the workmen. In just a few more days they'd be close enough to hear us and set us free. Then Jed would be history. At least now we had food. We'd survive, we'd make it. So I did nothing. I just sat there while he gave us a final evil grin, threw the bag between us then turned and left.

We managed to wait until the lock sounded on the outside shutter downstairs, before pouncing on the bag like ravenous wolves.

Grabbing a limp sandwich I crammed it into my mouth ripping out a huge chunk. My cheeks bulged as I struggled to chew the huge portion of bread and some sort of indistinguishable filling. Swallowing before I'd really chewed it, I bit off another piece about the same size and seconds later went through the same process with another sandwich. By the time I was on my third a stabbing pain had lodged itself right in the centre of my chest.

"I think I've eaten too fast," I groaned.

"You don't say," said Rebecca, her sarcasm back to full strength.

"I need a drink," I said, reaching into the bag. "How many sandwiches have you had?"

"I'm on my second because I'm actually chewing mine so I don't end up with indigestion."

"Smart Alec," I murmured.

"Aren't I?" Rebecca grinned, revealing pieces of chewed bread in her teeth.

"Eew! Shut your mouth," I said, grimacing, "I do not want to see your food, thank you very much."

"I don't see why not," Rebecca said, deliberately opening her mouth wide to reveal a mushed white paste on her tongue.

"Eeew! Put it away!" I swiped at her, hitting her arm before turning away.

"Too fussy, you are." Rebecca giggled, sending small white flecks spraying towards me.

"Oh, you're gross!" I said, but I didn't really mind. It was just so good to have food heading down into my stomach. Drinking several gulps of lemonade the blockage in my chest eased and I was ready to eat more.

"How many sandwiches has he brought?" I asked, my nose hanging over the edge of the carrier.

"Don't know," Rebecca answered, "But there seems to be plenty. Hope that doesn't mean he'll be ages before he comes back again."

"Oh, don't say that!" My recently consumed food flipped over in my stomach. "I don't want to be hungry ever again."

"Well, it wouldn't exactly be my choice either, but we're at that maniac's mercy." She peered into the bag. "We'd better stop now. We can have a couple more at supper then be careful again tomorrow in case he doesn't come back."

My new lighthearted feeling sagged like a kid being told Father Christmas might not find their house. I hated having to rely on somebody so unpredictable. He was a kidnapper and a wife beater, how could we rely on him for anything? He'd obviously got more than one screw loose.

148

"Rebecca?"

"Hmn?"

"Will anybody ever find us? I mean, all we've got now are the workmen. Will they ever be near enough?"

There was silence for a few minutes before Rebecca answered.

"Sure. They're getting closer every day. They'll be here eventually and you never know the police might keep an eye on Jed anyway. They might follow him here."

"Hmn, maybe." But my heart still hung heavy inside me.

***

The next day, being Sunday, was eerily quiet. No workmen came and goodness knows how far we were away from the nearest housing estate because no kids came around either. I know if I'd lived near a boarded up place like this when I was a kid I'd have been there all the time. It was perfect for playing 'hide and seek' and treasure hunting. I know there wasn't exactly any treasure, unless you counted me and Rebecca but an old boot or broken cup is treasure to any kid with an imagination.

"Anybody'd think he'd left us on the moon," I muttered, mainly just to make a noise.

"Wouldn't know; he drove far enough. But that's the reason for the van. Nobody could see us and we couldn't see where we were going."

"Not that it matters," I said, rattling the chain, "We're not exactly going anywhere anyway."

I looked down at my right ankle, peeling back the bra to peek beneath. It was still red and swollen but the cut had scabbed over and didn't hurt quite as much. Rebecca's doctoring wasn't too bad after all.

The day dragged on. There wasn't even the interlude of shouting at deaf workmen. We'd run out of ideas for 'I spy' days ago. I mean, a blank room and empty bathroom can only offer up so many ideas, no matter how imaginative you are. We'd talked about absolutely everything. I now knew the names of all Rebecca's friends from nursery upwards. I knew about her teeth trouble and her having five taken out when she was thirteen. I knew the names of all her boyfriends past and present. I even knew the name of her pet rabbit from when she was four! I'd told her all about me, which wasn't much. There was just nothing left to say.

"I'm gonna scream if we don't get out of here soon," I said, pacing.

"I'm gonna scream if you don't stop jangling that chain of yours," Rebecca snapped back. "It's like watching a flipping tennis match without any of the entertainment.

"Hey, if you can find a way to take it off, feel free, I'd love to lose it!" I mean, what was I supposed to do about the freaking chain? "With this thing on my leg, I can't exactly get out of your way either, can I?"

"Why don't you just sit down for a bit?" Rebecca frowned up from her usual position.

"I can't just sit there forever," I growled, "It's driving me nuts! That's all we do for hours and hours. I'm going crazy!"

I actually felt like pulling my hair out in frustration. I always thought it was a stupid thing to say, I mean, why would anybody want to pull their hair out? But right at that moment I just wanted to rip something apart and my hair was real handy.

"Well pace quietly," Rebecca snapped back.

"Why? It's quiet enough around here. Somebody's got to make some noise!"

"Why? Why can't it just be quiet? Sunday's supposed to be a day of rest, isn't it?"

"Every day's a rest day around here! I'm ready to move, walk, jump up and down. Anything!"

I jumped to prove my point then instantly regretted it when pain seared through my ankle as the anklet dug into the angry swollen skin.

"Aargh!" I cried and dropped onto the floor, cradling my leg.

"Are you okay?" Rebecca crawled over to me.

"It'll be right," I said, lifting the bra to watch droplets of blood leak from a break in the scab.

"I'm sorry, I didn't mean to wind you up," Rebecca said, softly, "It's just that I'm going as crazy as you are in my own way. When I'm frustrated I take it out on the nearest person and around here, you're it."

I smiled. "I'm sorry as well. Do you think if we stay here long enough, we'll end up hating each other?"

"Nah," Rebecca said, lightly. "Take a look at this face. Now how can you hate that?"

"You've got a point," I said, with a half smile. "If I hate you it'll be like hating myself."

"Exactly." She leaned back so that she was sitting in front of me, her hands propped behind her and her legs outstretched. "Although, I do think I'm prettier."

"Yeah, sure. I don't think so. We're identical."

"Yeah, but there's slight differences that make me more beautiful."

"Like what?"

Rebecca sat for a while, her head tilting left and right. "Well, that red bit on your neck, for a start."

151

"What red bit?"

"Oh, that one just below your ear," she said, pointing. "It's gonna be a whacking great zit, the size of Vesuvius."

"No!" I said, reaching up to feel.

"Gotchya!" She yelled then leapt up before I could slap her.

"Right, that's it!" I shouted and jumped up after her. Ignoring the pain in my ankle I chased her around the room, occasionally tripping over lengths of chain as we ran.

By the time we'd finished we were panting and the chains were hopelessly entangled. It took us another fifteen minutes of weaving in and out to undo the mess.

"My leg's bleeding again!" I called from the bathroom.

"Don't worry, Doctor Becs will look after you."

As the dim light dropped, we were both relieved to hear the lock rattle on the door. We were gonna be fed again. Moments later Jed appeared in the doorway, dropped the carrier bag then strode in a couple more steps, his eyes sparkling.

"I've brought food," he said, "But today you've got to earn it. I've been figuring, I'm doing all the work, traipsing back and forwards, making your precious sandwiches, taking all the risks and what do I get? A load of verbal, that's what."

"What do you want, thanks?" Rebecca snapped.

"Shh, Becs," I hissed. There was something different today, he'd come earlier than usual and his eyes glinted in the remaining light. It reminded me of Emma before she announced my adoption to me and the world.

"You both look so like my Marcy when she was your age," Jed said, his voice heavy and low.

I managed a gulp. Even Rebecca was silent.

"Do you know how much I hate that woman?"

I felt like my whole brain exploded. He hated her?

"But I thought you wanted her back?" I whispered.

"Oh, I do," he said. "She's my wife but she's got way out of hand. She's stolen years of my life putting me in that prison. Now she's going to come back to me. She's got to suffer a lot to make up for what she's done. Then, once she's learned her lesson we'll be okay again, just like before you came along. Now, talking of you, you've caused me a lot of trouble and you've only just started to pay."

Suddenly there wasn't enough air in the room.

"Do you know what you do when you hate people, but have to keep them around?" he asked, then grinned broadly. "No? You have some fun."

Reaching into his pocket he pulled out a crumpled piece of card then flicked his wrist, skimming it across to us.

It landed beside my right foot so I reached forward and picked it up without taking my eyes off Jed. The card was rough, sort of pockmarked. Opening it up I found Marcy staring back at me but her face was barely recognizable. The whole picture was a mass of holes all the size of a pin prick.

Jed moved and something in his hand glinted in the torchlight. I looked up from the picture and instantly knew the cause of the holes. In his right hand Jed held about six darts, lean and gleaming they pierced my mind with horror. Jed's smile reminded me of a lion who'd sighted his prey.

153

"Ready for some fun?" he taunted.

Rebecca jumped up.

"If you think you're throwing those at us, you've got another thing coming!" she yelled.

Jed lifted and dropped his hand, jiggling the darts. Even the gentle clatter of metal made my nerves tingle.

"What? You don't want to play?" he taunted.

I was stuck to the floor, I knew I should have been jumping up like Rebecca but none of my muscles worked. I couldn't believe he meant to throw darts at us.

"You try throwing even one of those and I'll …" Rebecca started.

"You'll what?" Jed jumped in, "Rattle your chains? Go on hunger strike? Come and attack me?" he chuckled. "Two steps back and I'm out of your range. A kick of this bag and I'll put you on hunger strike myself. Oh yeah, I remember, you've already been on one this week, haven't you? How many days without food was it?"

My mouth was totally dry. We were in the hands of a madman. I watched him enjoying tormenting us. Was this what a school bully turned into when they grew up? Or was he a victim who'd been bullied so much he now took sadistic pleasure hurting others?

"Anyway, who said anything about throwing them at *you*?"

Rebecca switched feet, obviously as confused as me.

I watched as Jed reached into his jacket pocket and pulled out some squares of paper. He flicked the first towards us. Rebecca picked it up, turned it over then stared at it in silence. She blinked fast, her fingers whitening as she gripped the edges.

"What is it, Becs?" I started to stand to look over her shoulder but another paper floated across the room and landed at my feet.

I frowned down at it, suddenly afraid to pick it up. Whatever it was had silenced Rebecca.

Swallowing hard I reached out, my hands actually shaking.

The paper was pretty thick and glossy, but there were a couple of pin pricks in it. Slowly I turned it over then gasped as every ounce of oxygen fled from my lungs. Luke's face, pale with a worried frown looked back at me; although not quite. His eyes were missing; they'd been stabbed out by darts. I couldn't breathe, my chest tightened. What did this mean? Was Jed going to hurt Luke? Had he hurt him already? Just seeing my beautiful boyfriend made my breath come in short gasps but his poor sad face and those empty eyes …

I panted, trying to suck in air as another paper landed beside me. I saw Rebecca bend down, pick it up and glance at it before handing it to me.

"You're sick!" she snapped, as another one landed at her feet.

As she bent to pick it up I looked at the new one in my hand and felt my eyes burn. Mum and Dad stood at our front door. They were so thin, their faces gaunt, with red rimmed eyes filled with so much pain. More pictures followed. Luke walking with his hands in his pockets, his shoulders hunched way down and his head hanging low. Mum and Dad on Queen Street hugging Rebecca's parents. Their eyes were filled with loss, their clothes hanging loose like they'd been washed too many times and gone baggy. I stared at them feeling like my heart was gonna explode.

The rattling of metal made me look up.

Jed, the sadistic jerk, was grinning broadly.

"Enjoying the photos? Thought you'd like to catch up on home life. Looks like both families are getting close, united in their grief. Poor people losing their little daughters, but you never were their daughters, were you? You're mine. Mine. They stole what didn't belong to them and now I've got you back and they'll pay!"

He swung his right leg back then kicked the food bag so hard it shot up in the air, spilling sandwiches and cans all over the room.

"It's time everybody understood, nobody messes with me. You, Marcy, your parents, that boyfriend of yours; I'm gonna make you all understand." He smiled. "Enjoy your photos and your food."

Then he turned and marched out through the doorway. I could hear his footsteps slowly receding and his voice floating back up to us.

"You'll all pay."

Even when he'd gone and all was silent, I still sat staring at the photos, each one stabbed with darts on their heads, chests or eyes.

"What's it all mean?" I eventually asked my voice no more than a whisper.

Rebecca sank slowly beside me, her back sliding down the wall, shaking her head. She clutched three pictures in her hands. One showed her brother Liam, his mouth open, shouting at someone out of view. Another showed her parents, even more gaunt than when I'd seen them. The other showed all our parents, walking down the steps outside Rebecca's house, holes where their eyes should be.

"They're so thin," she said, her voice distant.

"But what does it mean, Rebecca? Is he going to hurt our families?" I asked feeling like Jed had reached inside my chest and scooped out my heart.

"He's so sick," Rebecca mumbled. "I hope he's just talking about the ransom but I don't know. He's playing with our minds, trying to psych us out."

"He's succeeding," I said and drew in my arms, cradling the photos against my chest.

***

CHAPTER SIXTEEN

The next day was Monday, my ninth day in captivity. The workmen were back, but we'd slept late. We'd spent most of the night worrying, talking and shivering before finally sinking into an anxious sleep, riddled with nightmares.

We sat huddled on the floor, freezing. The jerk never did bring us any blankets.

***

"Did you hear a voice then?" I asked, about three o'clock. I sat perfectly still, not wanting to move incase the rattling of my chains covered any other voices.

"No."

"Are you sure?"

"Yes."

I looked down at Rebecca who sat slumped so low she was almost flat.

"Are you okay?"

"Oh, yeah, I'm fantastic, never better. Who wouldn't be after fifteen days in this flea pit being visited by a freaking madman?"

"I know, Becs but we're gonna get out of here." Heading across to the metal board, I pressed my ear to the cold surface listening intently. "I'm certain I heard

158

a voice. As soon as they've finished we're gonna bust our lungs shouting like mad and they're gonna hear us. They've just got to."

***

By four the machinery and crashing of masonry had almost fully quietened. It sounded like just one engine was still running.

"Becs! Come on, it's nearly time!" I urged.

Rebecca pushed herself up from the floor, the effort seeming almost too much for her.

"Ready?" I asked.

She nodded.

As soon as the last engine died, we started shouting.

"Help! Help, we're stuck in here! Help!"

Hammering on the metal between shouts we made a real racket. As the minutes passed I hammered louder, my shouts more desperate. Why didn't they come?

After fifteen minutes we knew there'd be no rescue that day.

"Tomorrow, Becs. They'll be nearer tomorrow."

"Yeah, sure."

I watched my twin sink back down onto the floor. Normally Rebecca was the cheerful, resilient one and I was the one who expected the worst, but somewhere in the last few days or even hours, we'd switched roles. I was trying to keep her spirits up instead of the other way around. Maybe the photos had been the final straw, knowing she might never see her family again. Fear swept up into my throat, squeezing tight. If Rebecca gave up, how much longer could I go on? It already felt like I was walking a daily tightrope of slim hope and I knew it would only take one more knock to tip me off completely.

The rest of the day passed and Rebecca didn't say another word. Even when I tried talking to her. She didn't even diss Jed when he dropped off the day's food parcel. He never said anything either. He just took a couple of steps into the room, threw the heavy carrier at us then left muttering something about getting a move on.

I ate a couple of sandwiches, but Rebecca wouldn't.

"Come on, you've got to eat, Becs," I urged, but she just looked at me and turned away. Within an hour she'd settled onto the floor and fallen asleep. I shivered, wrapping my dusty jacket further around me. How I wished for a hot shower, followed by a hot meal of spaghetti bolognaise, my favourite, then a scorching cup of coffee. I could almost smell the different aromas with my eyes closed and mouth watering.

When I opened my eyes the darkness hit hard and I sighed heavily. Every day the darkness descended earlier and seemed deeper than the night before.

With Rebecca already asleep, I settled down with a gap between us so as not to wake her. An icy November wind took advantage of every crack in the old building and swept around me all night, denying me sleep.

***

By the next morning every part of me felt stiff and achy. Rebecca stretched and groaned but when I offered her food she refused. By lunch time I was frantic.

"Becs, you're scaring me. Please eat something."

She sat against the wall, her legs drawn up and encircled by her arms. Her chin rested on her knees, eyes staring vacantly ahead.

"Rebecca! We're in this together and you're leaving me on my own!" I snapped, desperate to reach her.

"I'm still here," she murmured.

Hope tweaked at my heart, those were her first words since our shouting exercise the day before.

"Well you won't be for long, if you don't eat, will you? You're just being selfish!"

"What?" She actually raised her head and frowned at me.

"Well you are. As if I haven't got enough to worry about, now you're not eating and making it worse."

"Don't worry about me," she said, her head dropping down again.

Something flipped inside me and I shoved her hard in the side.

"Hey!" she objected.

"Hey, yourself!" I shouted. "You don't get it, do you? We're twins! You and me, we're the same. I see the image of me slouching there, not eating, fading away. Can't you see? I'm scared Becs, more scared than I've ever been in my whole life and right now there's only you and me. I need you. If you give up, it's like we've both given up. I see you thin, not eating, disappearing a bit more every day and I see it happening to me!"

Tears ran down my cheeks, I wanted to shake her, make her understand. She was my only hope, if we stood together there was a chance, but if Rebecca was gone, there was none. Right now she was a symbol of my life ebbing away.

Rebecca looked at me then her face crumbled.

"I'm sorry, Rach," she sobbed. "It just got so dark, on the inside, you know. Like there was nothing left. I've been listening to those workmen for over two weeks, longing for them to be near enough to hear me. When I was on my own it was like my whole existence depended on them, but they're never near enough. They're always another day away. Then seeing my mum, dad and Liam looking so devastated … I guess, I just gave up."

I reached out and we hugged our sobs merging. Her arm around my neck nearly cut off my oxygen, but I didn't care. She was talking, letting everything out. We were together again.

I don't know how long we sat there sobbing, but by the time the tears finally stopped I was exhausted. We separated and looked into each others' faces.

"Do I look as bad as you?" Rebecca asked.

"Well, if I've got red, blood-shot eyes, a snotty nose and swollen lips, then yeah, you look as bad as me."

A small smile slid across my twin's face. "I think we'd better clean up a bit then 'cause if those workmen hear us today, I don't want to be seen looking anything like you do right now."

I grinned back. Our situation hadn't changed but Rebecca was with me again, I didn't feel so alone and that made so much difference. I just hoped she was here to stay.

We stood together, arms around each others shoulders, marched forward then jammed in the bathroom doorway.

"You first," Rebecca said.

"Oh, no, you first, my lady," I said in a snooty voice.

"Oh, no, I would consider it an honour to let you go first," Rebecca said, with a little bow.

"Oh, all right then." I grinned and rushed in.

"Oy!" Rebecca shouted, running in and grabbing my arm. She pulled me back and rushed ahead to the sink.

"Oh, no you don't!" I said, grabbing her and pulling her back. I inched ahead.

"Uh, uh, me first." Rebecca gave such an almighty yank on my arm that I fell back, arms flailing. I couldn't stop myself and landed hard on the lino as Rebecca turned on the taps and began splashing her face.

"Loser!" she cried, between splashes.

I didn't really care. Rebecca was back!

***

We did our usual shouting exercise when everything fell silent but no one came. But they'd been so close we could actually tell the difference between the sounds made by the equipment and knew when to expect each crash of falling masonry. Within a couple of days we'd be found, I was certain.

As we gave up shouting for the day I watched Rebecca, my stomach twisting, hoping she wouldn't slip back into depression. She was silent for a couple of agonizing minutes then smiled up at me.

"Looks like it'll be tomorrow."

"Yeah," I said, hoping she could hang in there that bit longer.

***

Jed looked really full of himself when he arrived that evening.

"I've spoken to your mother today," he said.

"Janet?" I asked.

"No, Stupid," he growled. "Your real mother. She's gonna come back and live with me."

My lip twisted. Surely Marcy wouldn't do something that crazy?

"She wants to know whether you're alive," Jed continued.

So he'd used the blackmail. Us.

"Tell me something only you'd know," he said.

"Why should we?" Rebecca spat.

Jed leaned over her. "Because if you don't, you're no use to me at all, are you?" he said. "And one twin is cheaper to feed than two."

"What if neither of us helps you?" I asked, quickly.

"Then I take a trainer from you and a boot from her," he jabbed his foot towards Rebecca. "Still reeking with your B.O. Then you both disappear. No one will ever know what happened to you."

My heart beat slowed right down. I could feel every thump in my chest as I examined his outline, trying to work out whether he really meant it.

"What about ransom, I thought you wanted us for that?" Rebecca challenged.

Good one. I looked across at my twin silhouetted by the light of Jed's torch. With her chin raised in defiance she looked more like her old self.

"You weren't listening the other day, were you? Or has the cold addled your brain?" Jed laughed like he'd told this huge joke. "I only need your jackets for that. Once I've got Marcy convinced, I post the jackets to your parents. They drop off loads of money some place lonely, then me and my Marcy's got us a nice little nest egg to start our new life. Once she's back in my hands she'll do exactly as I say, I'll make sure of that. There'll be no getting away from me this time."

164

I didn't like the sound of that, at all. Marcy would have to love us a lot to go back to a maniac like that.

"It's up to you. If you don't help me then maybe I'll go visit those families of yours once they've paid up. You've seen how close I can get to them … Who knows what could happen? Life is so full of accidents."

Someone shoved a tennis ball down my throat. I looked at Rebecca and she nodded, we both knew he was crazy enough to do anything.

"All right, what do you want to know?" Rebecca's voice sounded strangled like she had her own tennis ball lodged next to her larynx.

Jed grinned, triumphantly.

"Tell me something so she'll know I've talked to you," he said.

"Well, tell her from me that if she gets back with you then she's a total loser and I definitely never want anything to do with her!" Rebecca snapped, producing a snarl from Jed.

"And you?" he growled, looking at me.

My brain went into overdrive. What could I say so she'd know it was me?

"Erm, tell her … I like her sunny kitchen."

Jed's top lip curled.

"You'd better be telling me straight or you'll pay!" With a last glare he dropped the carrier and headed out.

I watched his wide rear disappear then whispered, "I hope we didn't just make a mega mistake."

"We had no choice."

I knew she was right.

Neither of us spoke for ages. I kept imagining Jed's next appearance and what he might do. Shuddering, I pushed the thought from my mind.

"So what delectable delights are in the bag today?" Rebecca asked, breaking the silence at last.

Grateful for the distraction, I hutched forward and hooked my hand around the plastic handles pulling it towards us.

"Smells like ham and something mushy sandwiches and cola, again. I'm gonna look like a can of cola."

"You already do."

"Well if I do, you do too."

Rebecca's eyes narrowed. "I can never get away with that with you. It's a real pain being identical. I am thinner than you though, so I'll be a bottle of cola and you'll be a can."

"Gee thanks, Sis. I love you too." We were trying to be normal, to ignore the ever present threat, but it was all an illusion and Bec's comments about my shape stung. Although, if we hung around being half starved by Jed for much longer, my weight wouldn't be a problem anymore.

***

"I wonder how Jed got on with Marcy?" I mused the next morning.

"Nowhere, if she's got any sense."

I chewed my thumb nail. My friend Becca might have moved away but her habit had stayed with me.

"Which will be better for us, do you think?" I wondered.

Rebecca looked at me, her brown eyes serious.

"I don't think it looks good for us either way, Rach."

Her words hit me like rock, slamming the air out of my lungs.

"But, if she goes to him, that'll buy us a bit more time, won't it? I mean, she might ask more questions? Or if she's undecided, he might keep us around longer to try and persuade her? But if she says no, will he … you know … do something to us straight away, or keep us a bit just in case?"

Rebecca shrugged.

"Look, Rach. It doesn't make much difference. Unless we can make those workmen hear us within the next couple of days I reckon it's all over anyway."

My throat closed up tight, my eyes stinging.

"We've got to get rescued Becs, we can't die here. Not like this! We're only fifteen!"

Until then I'd been trying to convince myself that Jed was only making empty threats but on the inside I'd always suspected there was nothing empty about them. Now Rebecca had confirmed it. I tried to breathe but nothing happened. Clutching my twin, I gasped for air but there was none. My lungs hurt. I remembered the feeling. It happened on Armthorpe Road, back in Doncaster when I thought I'd lost Rebecca for good. Hyperventilating that's what the old man called it, but knowing its name didn't help.

"Rebecca!" I gasped, squeezing her arm.

I thrust my head down between my knees trying to make my lungs work. In the narrow gap, I saw Rebecca shuffle forwards.

"Calm down, Rach. Breathe steady, it's only a panic attack. I'm sorry, I shouldn't have upset you. It'll be all right. We'll find a way. Just breathe steady. Take deep breaths."

What do you think I'm trying to do? my brain screamed, but my lips stayed silent, there wasn't

167

enough air to speak. My lungs were killing me, begging for oxygen, but it just wouldn't get past my straw-like throat. It was like somebody had superglued my windpipe. My chest screamed with pain. I was gonna die, I knew I was gonna die. My grip on Rebecca's arm was so tight, she'd probably end up covered in bruises but I wouldn't be there to see them.

"Breathe, Rach!" Rebecca urged. "Come on, the air's there, just breathe. Slow and steady, one breath at a time."

Yeah, like I could take more than one at once.

"Come on, Rach! Breathe in. Hold it. Breathe out. Wait. Now breathe in, go on, breathe in. Now hold it. Now breathe out. Okay, steady, don't gasp. Breathe in again. Hold it. Now out again."

Slowly my lungs filled again, the pain easing. I loosened my grip on Rebecca, then let go. I saw her rub the red patch with her other hand.

"Sorry," I murmured.

"It's all right. It's my fault," she said, "I'd given up again. I shouldn't have. I'm real sorry, Rach."

I nodded. "It's okay."

The air suddenly exploded with the sound of motors firing, real close. My head shot up.

"How did we miss their cars arriving?" I asked, devastated. We couldn't afford to miss an opportunity to reach help.

"Er, we were otherwise occupied," Rebecca answered. If she was disappointed she was hiding it well.

"I can hear their voices."

We tilted our heads, sitting like two little puppies trying to distinguish sounds. A shout, I definitely heard it. Not loud enough to tell what it said but the voice definitely reached us.

"They're nearly here!" I yelled. Hope burst in my chest like a firework. Jumping up, I ran over to the metal shutter.

"Hey! We're here! Help us!" I shouted, banging on the freezing metal.

"Rach," Rebecca's cool hand rested on my shoulder. "They can't hear you. Their equipment's too loud." She talked like I was a three-year-old and suddenly I felt like one.

"Pretty stupid, hey?" I said with an embarrassed smile. "They just sound so *close*."

Rebecca grinned. "They are. We've got to be ready. When those machines get turned off and the rubble stops falling at the end of the day, we shout like our lives depend on it. Okay?"

"Okay." I nodded, because our lives really did depend on it.

***

CHAPTER SEVENTEEN

That day was the noisiest so far, the sound of bricks falling and metal objects crashing into buildings was deafening. The day dragged more than any of the others, the sense of urgency so strong. We both knew we didn't have long with Jed now that he'd given proof to Marcy and especially now the workmen were so close. He wouldn't want us to be discovered. The next twenty four hours could be our last chance. We knew there wouldn't be many more.

I ate the manky sandwiches because I knew I needed to but they felt like cardboard in my throat. I just wanted evening to come when we could shout and be rescued.

"What time is it?" I asked for the twentieth time.

"It's nearly four," Rebecca answered. "Just like it was two minutes ago. You have got your own watch, you know."

"We'd better get to the window," I said, ignoring her dig. "It's raining today, you never know, they might knock off early."

It was gloomy. The dark room had barely any light all day. I hurried over to the window, desperate not to miss what could be our last chance.

The machinery was so loud they had to be only a few doors away now.

"Come on, Rebecca!" I urged. Not able to understand her lack of urgency.

She groaned but slowly joined me on guard beside the grey shutter, the emblem of our captivity.

"It's going quiet," I hissed. As one after another the motors shut down and the sound of falling rubble finally stilled. "Voices, I can hear voices!" I yelled. "Help! Help us, we're in here!"

"Help!" Rebecca joined me, banging on the metal.

"HELP!" Our voices yelled in unison. "Let us out of here, we're trapped!"

Why weren't they coming? I'd heard their voices. They were distant and indistinguishable, but I'd definitely heard them.

"HELP!" I screamed, my throat tearing in pain, "HELP!"

Hammering on the metal, my fists were so cold that pain seared up my arms with every blow but I didn't care, I had to make them hear.

"HELP!"

Car doors slammed.

"NO! DON'T GO! HELP!"

Cars coughed into life.

"Why can't they hear us? HELP US!"

"It's no good Rach, they're gone." Rebecca shook her head, her hand on my shoulder. She always seemed to be trying to calm me.

"But they've got to hear us!" I swiped at my cheeks suddenly realising they were wet with tears. "They've just got to." My voice cracked and I sagged like a plastic bag dropped by the wind.

171

"We'll try again tomorrow," Rebecca said softly. "We'll make sure we're up early so we don't miss the opportunity."

"But what if we're not here in the morning?"

"We will be," she said. But she couldn't know that. Neither of us could.

Dragging myself over to our usual position on the opposite wall, I dropped to the floor, wasted. What if that was our last chance?

The day just got darker from then on, the dismal weather matching my mood. Rain pounded on the metal sheeting and it became impossible to see.

The storm was so loud the first sign of Jed's presence was his torch beam lighting up the empty doorway. My whole body stiffened. I sat rigid, staring at the corner of the room where the door should be. The light strengthened, entering the room but I couldn't see Jed. The torchlight hit my eyes and I slammed them shut, the brightness, excruciating.

Jed didn't speak but I heard his footsteps cross the room and stop in front of Rebecca. I still couldn't see him, blinded by the torchlight. Then the beam hit the floor, he'd put the torch down. Why? What was he doing?

"Ow!" I heard Rebecca shout. "Get off me!"

Squinting in the glare I could just make out Jed's hands on her ankles.

"Oi! What're you doing?" I demanded. "Leave her alone!"

Pain shot through my left cheek and jaw as his fist slammed into my face, snapping my head to the right. Tears sprung from my eyes, my face feeling like I'd run into a wall.

"Keep still!" he growled.

"What are you doing to her?" I demanded, terrified he'd hit me again but equally scared for Rebecca.

There was a metallic snapping sound then Rebecca screamed.

"Let go of me!"

I could hear her struggling.

"What're you doing?" I cried, trying to stand. "Let her go!"

"Oomph!" Jed groaned. Then I heard a thud and a gasp from Rebecca. I could just make out her shape across the room near the bathroom door.

"You're coming with me!" Jed ordered. "And quit struggling or I'll kill your sister!"

I froze, half way to my feet.

I could see the shapes struggling and heard Rebecca groan again.

"I'm warning you!" Jed growled.

I cursed the dark, wishing I could see what was happening. Dropping to my hands and knees I reached for the torch. Clumsily I grasped it and managed to turn it enough to make out Jed's large figure and Rebecca pulling away.

"Go on, Rebecca, run! Get help!" I shouted, "Oomph!" The air exploded out of my lungs as Jed's hard boot slammed into my ribs sending my crashing back into the wall.

The torch flicked out of my hand towards the stairs. Spinning, it showed Jed pulling a struggling Rebecca towards him, then clamping his great arms around her waist, trapping her backwards against his left side. She bucked and kicked but his grip was secure. My chest burned, oxygen reluctant to refill my lungs, but I scrambled to my feet and made a dive for them. I wasn't quick enough.

"REBECCA!" I screamed as she was dragged from the room. "Rebecca!"

Minutes later, I heard the metal shutter slam downstairs but didn't hear the lock. It didn't matter, I wasn't going anywhere.

"NO!" Screams filled my whole body, bursting out in an anguished wail. He'd taken my sister. He'd dragged her away in front of me and I didn't stop him. He was gonna kill her, then he'd come back for me. I knew he'd come back for me.

My jacket felt cold and damp against my face, soaked with tears. My cheek and ribs throbbed with pain but that was nothing to the pain in my heart. I'd rather have faced Emma and her evil little grin every day of my life than watch my twin being dragged away to her death.

I rocked, backwards and forwards; waiting. I had no comprehension of time passing, no idea how long I sat. I only knew my time would come. No one could help, no one would rescue me now. I'd follow Rebecca and that would be the end. Would it be quick or slow? How much would it hurt? There was no escaping now, the metal chains would hold me until he was ready to release me and take me away.

How had he done that? How had he released Rebecca's chain? My mind slowly lifted from the despairing fog. What if he'd dropped whatever it was in the struggle? I shuffled over to the discarded torch. His hands had been too busy trying to hold Rebecca to pick it up. I slowly shone it across the whole room then back again. Nothing. Standing, I headed into the bathroom, maybe whatever it was had been kicked in there in the struggle?

The light picked out the old bathtub, toilet and sink. I even shone it into the bath and behind the door but there was nothing.

The stairs. What if it had dropped on the stairs? Hurrying over, I shone the torch onto the landing then down each step, slowly, one at a time. The first, second, third. Onto the fourth, fifth, sixth, seventh. I stopped. Something had glinted on the sixth step. Returning the beam, I slowly examined it again.

My breath caught. There was definitely something down there. It was tucked right to the back with only a small shiny piece in sight. It was impossible to make out what it was but I had to hope. It was a long way down about as far as the bag had been. My ankle throbbed at the memory of that experience but I had to try, it was my only hope.

Shutting out the thought that this time there was no Rebecca to help if I slipped, I laid flat and slithered out onto the landing. Every nerve tingled as I put all my weight onto my arms and descended one step at a time. By the time I'd reached the fourth step my arms were shaking with the strain. Only my ankles were still in the room above and once they fully turned the corner my whole weight would be on my wobbly arms.

Taking a deep breath, I lifted my right hand and dropped it onto the fifth step. My ankles slid onto the landing. It felt like my heart left my chest and jumped into my throat.

It took several deep breaths before I dared lift my left arm and drop it down beside my right. I lurched forwards, gasping but didn't fall. All I had to do now was reach down and pick up that object. I just hoped it was a pair of pliers. I'd positioned the torch on the landing but now my body was blocking the light, casting a shadow onto the step below and making it impossible to see anything down there.

Using every gram of concentration, I lifted my right hand but my left arm wobbled so much, I quickly put it back down again.

"Come on," I urged, my voice thick with the tension and pressure of being upside down. I braced myself again, then lifting my hand I reached down.

"WHAT'RE YOU DOING!" Jed's voice boomed into the silence.

My left arm crumpled with shock and I plunged down.

"Aargh!" I screamed as my whole body weight slammed onto my right ankle.

Jed rushed up, grabbing my shoulders, taking the strain.

"Is this what you wanted?" His voice was filled with amusement as he picked up the pliers and held them in front of my face. "Looks like I got back just in time."

I wanted to struggle but I couldn't. Any movement was excruciating and if I escaped his grasp I was sure my ankle would snap.

Pushing me up before him he slowly climbed the stairs. When I was almost in a sitting position, he reached forwards and using the pliers, snapped through the chain.

This was my chance. I could push with my legs and force him to fall backwards. It might kill him, probably me too, but did it matter if I was gonna die anyway? But then I thought of Rebecca. If I died now I'd never know what happened to her. I had to at least find out that much. So I didn't struggle. I let him drag me backwards down the stairs. He half carried me across the room I'd last seen eleven days before. My arm scraped on the metal shutter as he dragged me through, but I didn't care. It didn't matter any more.

Rain pelted down, drenching me as he dragged me like a window dummy to his van and threw me in. The door slammed shut, resonating inside the hollow interior. This was it and there was no fight in me, not like on the journey there. Somewhere inside my mind I knew I should be fighting, screaming, shouting, but it was like all the energy had been sucked out of me. Maybe it was seeing Rebecca dragged out that way. If she couldn't escape, what chance did I have? I'd just ruined my best opportunity by being too slow and weak. My wobbly arms wouldn't support me. Why hadn't I ever done keep fit? Now I'd never get the chance.

I don't know how long the journey lasted. I could hear water sloshing under the tyres and knew the rain was still falling. It seemed to fit somehow, pouring rain and darkness for my last night on earth.

After a sharp left turn the van finally stopped. It tipped as Jed clambered out of the driving seat and opened the side door. My eyes, so used to the dark could make out an open space with a mass of trees close by. Jed grabbed my right arm and dragged me to the door then clamping his tree trunk arm around my waist he lifted me out. My feet barely even touched the floor as he lumbered across the open space, his boots squelching in the mud. His was the only vehicle in the car park.

I was instantly soaked, the cold rain running down my face. After being trapped inside for so long the feeling of something so natural felt good, slowly reaching and awakening my soul. My mind emerged from its haze as Jed half dragged, half carried me through a sort of gateway. I could just make out the words 'Melton Wood' carved into a tall post beside the entrance. I tried to grab the fence as we passed through but was too late. As trees closed in around us torchlight shone out. Jed must've kept a second torch in his van. My view was behind and my eyes, so used to the dark, watched the car park recede into the distance. We were on a proper path surrounded by thick tree trunks with branches almost bare of leaves. The rain didn't fall as rapidly under here but the drops were huge, rolling off the few remaining leaves.

My weight must have got too much for Jed as he finally let me down, his hand fiercely gripping my right arm. He didn't even pause in his stride but kept right on going, dragging me along. Fallen wet leaves covered the path, centimetres deep in places. My heart pounded, if I was to get away this was my chance. If I didn't escape now I could be dead real soon, but if I got away I might never know what happened to Rebecca. If she was still alive I was her only hope. My mind was a mess. What was I supposed to do? Jed was a mad man, he'd probably already killed Rebecca and I was next but she was my twin and if there was any chance of saving her, I had to take it.

I hardly noticed our route as I fought my own internal battle.

Suddenly branches scratched my arms and weeds wrapped around my ankles. He'd gone off the path! The undergrowth was thick and the trees close together. Every nerve sparked into life. This was it, he was going to kill me here and in all this foliage, who would find me? Maybe a dog in a few days would come snuffling around.

As he bent low, I dug my nails deep into his arm.

"No!" I cried, struggling. "Let me go! Where's Rebecca? What have you done with her?"

"Aargh!" he cried, viciously pulling me in to him. His arms wrapped around my waist, squeezing tightly.

I groaned as my insides twisted. But it didn't stop me struggling, there was no way I was gonna give in easily.

Despite my efforts he managed to lift up some sort of board. It must have been covered in soil or leaves because I'd never noticed it. Underneath was a shallow dark hole.

As Jed stepped down into it, I found my legs spread out in a sitting position on the cold damp earth with my back still pressed against him. From that position there was little I could do except twist around and watch as he leaned forwards, tugging at something. His torchlight picked out another wooden cover fastened securely with a heavy bolt. It was this stiff bolt that was the focus of his attention. Cursing, he laid the torch down so he could use his full hand.

He's going to bury me! The thought shot into my brain sending electric currents surging through my body.

"NO!" I cried. "No way, you're not putting me down there!"

I writhed and twisted, managing to bend forwards and bite the back of his hand.

"Aargh!" he cried, his grip loosening momentarily but as I pulled away, his grip tightened again, pulling me violently back.

"Let me go!" I cried, digging my feet into the ground and trying to lever myself away.

"Pack it in!" he yelled as a fierce pain exploded in my skull.

179

My whole body went limp, stars flashing in my eyes. If it was only his fist that'd hit me, it was a powerful one. My senses spun and I couldn't think. Somewhere inside my head I knew I had to move, but it was like my brain was cut off from the rest of my body. Every limb was limp and lifeless, no messages were getting through. My heart tripped, desperately trying to encourage my body into life, but nothing responded.

I heard a grating sound and felt his body lift. He must have succeeded in releasing the bolt and uncovering the hole. I'd be dragged in there next and there was nothing I could do to stop it happening. Straightening up, his other arm wrapped around my waist pulling me in. My useless legs dragged across the damp earth. There was no ground under me any more I was over the hole and would be in there any second. My brain screamed for me to act but it was like one of those nightmares when you're terrified but totally unable to move. Only this was no dream it was very serious reality.

"Run!" I heard a shout, but where from? My fuddled mind tried to process it. The voice sounded familiar. Who was supposed to run? How? Where?

"Rachel! Run!"

Suddenly Jed's body tipped and fell. He dropped into the upper hole, dragging me after him.

His arms flailed and I suddenly found myself free. Instinct made me reach out, desperately trying to grip onto something to stop my descent.

My eyes, so used to the dark, spotted a tree root jutting out of the ground and I grabbed it.

My upper body descent stopped but my feet still slid a few more centimetres before finally finding a foothold. I pulled with every ounce of energy I had and levered myself out of the hole.

"YOU…!" Jed's voice boomed as he came to rest on the ledge above the lower hole but he wasn't looking at me, he was looking down through his trap door.

A small face with wide eyes and upturned nose peered up out of the gloom.

"Run, Rach!" it urged. "Run, now!"

"Rebecca!" I gasped.

"Go!" she screamed.

"But I can't leave you!" Rebecca was alive, she was down in that dark pit surrounded by walls of black earth. I had to get her out.

Jed was already lifting himself up. As he managed to stand, he kicked out at Rebecca's face. She ducked, narrowly missing the impact.

"Run, Rach! You're our only chance!" she yelled.

I saw her reach up and try to grab Jed's boot to hinder him.

I ran. Disoriented from the blow to my head and being dragged through the woods, I had no sense of direction. Away from Jed was the only way I knew. My mind raged as a lump the size of a fist lodged in my throat. I felt like a coward running away, leaving my twin to fight a battle she couldn't win. I should have stayed, fought with her, rescued her from that pit. But what if I failed? Then we'd both die. My running for help was our only hope, our last chance, or was it? Was I condemning Rebecca by leaving? If anything happened to her I'd never forgive myself. I stopped running, desperate to make the right decision, should I keep going and find help or should I go back?

Tears mixed with the cold rain on my face as I debated. I had to make the right choice; both our lives depended on it. Twigs snapped behind me and my decision was made. Jed was coming. I set off again, old leaves squelching beneath my feet and weeds brushing my legs. My ears tweaked, listening to the other heavy set of feet. They were gaining on me. My skin prickled, my soaked clothes clinging to me as I desperately ran on. Running for my life, our lives, but what if Rebecca was already dead? He wouldn't have just left her. Had he only closed and locked the hatch or had he hurt her?

My heart pounded and I shook my head, I couldn't think like that, I just had to keep going.

Branches lashed against my face and arms, my thin jacket no protection against their fury as I forced them aside. Nettles stung my legs, a few making it through my thick jeans, but I had no time to think about them. Strangely my ankle didn't hurt maybe it was adrenaline keeping me going. I remembered limping with the first few steps and wondering how I'd outrun him but after a few minutes I stopped noticing. I ran blindly, it all looked the same, tall tree trunks, bushes and brambles.

Suddenly my foot slipped on wet leaves, I fought to stay upright but it was no good. Crashing to the ground, icy water splashed up into my face filled with small pieces of debris. Hoping it was bits of earth and not insects, I shuddered but pushed myself up and ran on, listening for Jed's footsteps.

How close was he? I'd lost precious time with that fall.

His strides were longer than mine, but he was bigger and older. An occasional flicker of light told me he still had his torch and wasn't far behind. I was relying solely on my eyes' long adjustment to the dark to find my way.

Finally the trees broke and I ran out onto a path. More trees lined the opposite side so I frantically scanned left and right. Which way? A wrong decision could lead me deeper into the woods and I desperately wanted to find my way out. I chose right but within metres I'd reached a crossroads.

Now which way? A tall stone column stood guard at either side of me as I quickly scanned. If I went right, I'd be going back the way I came, towards Rebecca, but could I find her again? The path ahead was too narrow, it could fade out. Left could lead out of the woods and towards help. No idea whether I was making the right choice I turned left and ran, cringing as my feet sloshed through a puddle. Icy water washed over and into my trainers.

"Eew!" I groaned as they squelched beneath me.

Jed's footsteps still crunched behind me, but were they fading? I hardly dared hope but they did seem a little way behind, maybe my youth and school sports were paying off? The path suddenly ended and once more I was left with a choice. Did this wood never end? For no real reason I took the left turn this time, hoping I wasn't doubling back on myself. There had to be a road somewhere, Jed had just driven along one, but where was it?

My lungs felt like they were going to explode and my legs screamed for me to stop. I obeyed. Bending to rest my hands on my knees, I listened, panting furiously. Wind whipped the remaining leaves sending a shower of water down on me. It was only then I realised the rain had actually stopped. An owl screeched nearby making me clutch at my heart. With trees looming on every side and the constant threat of Jed catching me, my senses were on high alert. The snap of a twig on my right was enough to set me running again. I could've been a squirrel, a rabbit or Jed but I wasn't waiting around to find out.

Suddenly the trees fell back, opening into a small clearing. Facing me were four paths, branching off like spokes in a wheel. I stood in the fifth spoke trying to figure out which way to go. Small wooden benches stood between each of the junctions and I longed to sit down and rest but couldn't. Jed may not be far behind and if he'd gone back to Rebecca … I couldn't think about it. I had to get help quick.

Straight ahead, Rachel. If you keep going in as straight a line as possible you're bound to come out somewhere, I told myself.

None of the paths were exactly straight ahead but I picked the nearest to it and set off again. My feet pat-patted on the compacted earth, occasionally sliding in patches of mud.

I passed what looked like some sort of clearing on my right then suddenly I was out. I'd run between two cement posts and the wood was behind me. My throat filled up and I swallowed hard trying not to be swamped by tears of relief. Peering through the dark, I could make out a narrow path leading through a field. There were low crops on both sides, probably already cut down for the winter. Thankfully they were still tall enough to show the way. It was a bit lighter out here. Looking back there was no sign of Jed so I allowed myself a rest. My lungs had never hurt so much and my leg muscles were excruciating, but with Rebecca relying on me I couldn't stop for long.

Cold wind blew around me now there were no trees to offer protection and despite the heat from my running, I shivered. Jogging on I finally came to a fork in the path. I stood, listening for sounds of traffic but although I could hear cars somewhere I couldn't tell the direction, maybe both. I turned right. So far my instincts had paid off, leading me out of the wood. I just hoped this guess was right as well. I walked for some way before being surrounded by trees again.

No! my brain screamed, I couldn't take being lost in a wood again! But then I spotted a big bolder and beyond that, a road.

"Yes!" I cried, before quickly looking back. Clamping my mouth shut, I looked left and right. There was no pavement to walk on, just the road with weeds on either side. The left hand side sloped steeply up towards the field I had just left. I seemed to be high up on a hill and near the bottom I could see a few lights.

"Houses!" A sob escaped. I was nearly there. Turning left, I followed the road, looking longingly at those lights way down the hill. Spotting a narrow path leading from the other side of the road directly to the houses, I stopped. The path appeared to cross open fields. It'd be quick and Jed might not see me, but if he did, there'd be no chance of anybody coming to my aid. The road was the longer route and Jed was more likely to find me but there was also the chance of a passing driver helping me. I shivered, suddenly remembering the last driver, Jed, pulling me into his van. Why wasn't anything easy?

My brain swam with options, but before I decided my ears tweaked. A car. Headlights came from behind me. My heart sped up with a mixture of fear and hope as I waved my arms.

"Help! Help me!"

A cold blast of air hit me and icy water sprayed up my legs as the car sped past.

"Thanks a bunch!" I yelled after it.

Pushing away the negative thoughts that screamed for me to just collapse and give up, I headed off down the road, the path forgotten.

A few minutes later another set of headlights approached on the opposite side. The engine roared and sounded like an old banger or a souped up exhaust.

Stepping into the middle on my side of the road I waved my arms and the blue fiesta screeched to a stop.

"Hey, Babe! You want some?" A hail of male laughter burst from the car. "Come on, Babe, you're hot and we're ready!"

I stepped back.

"Hey, come on, we're waiting!" The horn honked loudly, repeatedly.

"No, it's okay," I said, backing right onto the verge away from them.

"Hey! You signaled us. We not good enough for ya?" His voice now hard and aggressive the driver opened his door. A booted foot stepped out and a closely shaved head emerged, with a deep frown over dark eyes.

Wrapping my arms across my chest, I looked left and right, longing for another car to appear.

"Leave her MJ, the girls are waiting," another voice persuaded.

"Yeah," MJ agreed then pointing at me, he scowled. "You watch it. You're begging for trouble."

The head disappeared and his door clicked shut. Seconds later the engine roared and the car sped off.

Tears spilled down my cheeks. I thought I was safe away from Jed but now even on the road, I was in danger. Was it all my fault? Rebecca's dad thought it was. Would Rebecca be safe now if it wasn't for me?

Had I caused all this? But how? All I ever wanted was to get on with everybody.

Wiping my eyes I set off jogging again, I had no choice.

Several more cars passed but I'd lost my courage. My only hope was the houses at the bottom of the hill. I hoped one would be an old person's bungalow where I'd be safe and could phone the police.

Another car pulled close behind me.

Go past, I silently urged, not daring to look back. *Go past!*

The car stopped and my back tingled like a thousand spiders were running down it as I heard a door open. Tensing, I braved a look over my shoulder. Through the glare of the headlights I made out a white vehicle and the silhouette of a bulky male figure. Jed had found me. Fear jumped into my throat and exploded in a scream. I set off running, but how could I outrun that van? Every nerve in my body sparked like an electric current coursing through me.

"Miss! Miss! Can I help you? Are you in trouble?"

I paused. That voice wasn't Jed. I turned but continued to back away. The man was in dark clothes.

"Miss, it's the police, we had a call about a girl trying to flag down cars. Are you in trouble?"

I looked again, finally realising the dark clothes were actually a black uniform. My knees buckled and I sank down onto the tarmac.

Within seconds the policeman was at my side.

"Are you all right, Love?"

I couldn't speak the sobs were too hard, too strong. The officer put his arms around me and I clung to him.

"Come, on. Let's get you into the warmth of the car." He helped me up and started back to the vehicle, but I grasped his arm, stopping him.

"Rebecca," I managed.

"Rebecca?"

I nodded. "My sister, Rebecca, he's still got her in the wood."

"There's another girl in the wood?" the officer repeated.

I nodded again, "My sister. Jed's got her in a hole. I think he'll kill her." My voice cracked and I couldn't go on.

"Right." The officer's voice sounded deeper, more commanding. "Come with me. Mike, radio it in. We've got another girl in the woods. Possibly in immediate danger. We need back up. What's your name, young lady?"

"Rachel Brooks."

Recognition lit his face.

"The missing twins?"

I nodded.

"Mike, tell them it's the missing twins. Tell them to contact the parents." My bottom lip wobbled at the mention of my parents, but I bit it, hard. I had to hold it together now for Rebecca.

The couple of minutes it took to radio it in seemed like an age but finally the other officer left the car, carrying two huge torches.

"Right, young lady, lead us in."

All the aches left my legs, adrenaline and hope took its place as I lead the officers back up the road and onto the path. My stomach flipped over when we reached the edge of the woods, but I couldn't let fear stop me. I was here to help Rebecca.

The path through the trees was much clearer now with the beams from two powerful torches. We reached the five spokes quickly, but that's when I stopped. I knew the path wasn't the one on my immediate right or left but which of the other two was it?

"Do you know the way?" The officer's voice sounded gruff, all of a sudden, or was it just the blood rushing through my ears? Rebecca was depending on me and I hadn't a clue which way to go.

"Just a minute," I said. I stood there trying to think but I just couldn't. Walking over to each one in turn, I stood facing the officers. "It's this one," I said finally.

"Are you sure?"

I shook my head. "Not exactly, but it's the best I can do." I looked up at him. "I have to be right."

We set off down the path. I wanted to run but the officers kept up a steady pace, their strides long and determined.

"I think it's down here," I said, when we came to a fork on the right. I chewed my thumb nail, hoping I was going the right way. I mean, I'd been terrified and just ran. I didn't exactly take time to mark my route and this place was so big. If I was wrong, how would we ever find Rebecca and that deadly hole?

We'd walked for sometime when I suddenly felt like dancing.

"There! The two cement pillars. I remember them!" I ran up to them and actually stroked the nearest. "This is it. I came down here."

I lead them so far up then looked towards my left.

"I came from somewhere in there," I said, pointing into the bushes and trees. "My sister's in there somewhere."

"Do you know where?" The officer shone his torch between the trees as the other one panned his left and right along the path.

My joy disappeared like a snowdrop melting in a warm hand.

"I think I ran in a straight line," I said uncertainly.

The officer tilted his radio up towards his mouth. "We need the dogs," he said.

More delay. We didn't even set off through the trees we had to wait for the dogs to arrive. A unit must have already been on their way because it only took about ten minutes, but those ten minutes felt like ten hours to me.

"Wait here," the burly officer said as two large Alsatians with their handlers set off crunching through the undergrowth.

"No!" I couldn't believe it, they couldn't expect me to wait there. "My sister's in there. I've got to help find her!"

Rushing forwards, I suddenly felt strong hands on my shoulders.

"Wait here," a firm voice said. "It's for the best. Let them do their job."

I struggled a bit but suddenly my energy was gone. Inside I knew why they wanted me to wait. They thought Rebecca might be dead and they didn't want me to see. Leaning back against the officer, I didn't even know which one, I watched the torch light flicker in and out between the trees then fade into the distance.

Silence filled the woods. Only the occasional bark from the dogs and the rustle of a lonely leaf broke the silence. Even the remaining two officers were quiet. Every so often their radios crackled into life but I couldn't understand a word of it. Understanding the garbled crackle must take years of experience. Neither the male or female responded to the radios so I guessed it wasn't information for them. One of them produced a blanket from somewhere and wrapped it around my shoulders. I gathered it in around my neck, it gave me something to hold on to. The officer had let me go some time ago, once he'd figured I wasn't gonna rush off into the wood and give them somebody else to search for.

The night suddenly erupted with the sound of excited barking. My head snapped up.

"They've found her!" I surged forwards, but hands clamped my shoulders again.

"Wait here."

"But they've found her!" I looked up, pleading. The officer's dark eyes were filled with pity. "You think she's dead. Don't you?"

"We don't know yet," the female officer stepped closer, her voice soft, reassuring. It didn't work.

My teeth closed tightly around my bottom lip and I bit hard. I could taste blood but didn't care. Somehow the pain helped. I watched the blackness through the trees, nothing moved.

The radios crackled.

The male officer, tipped his towards his mouth. "Affirmative," he said.

I looked at him expectantly and felt a wave of relief as he smiled.

"They've found her, she's alive."

***

191

CHAPTER EIGHTEEN

The small 'Quiet Room' of Doncaster Royal Infirmary's children's ward was warm and comfortable. Sitting on a brown faux leather settee I could feel the gentle heat slowly reaching my frozen bones. A cup of hot tea burned my fingers but I hugged it like a life jacket. Mum sat beside me, so much thinner than she'd been eleven days ago. Her hand rested on my lap. She'd never let go of me since she and Dad had come into the room an hour earlier.

***

A police officer had been sitting with me when the door opened and Mum and Dad came in, their faces gaunt but eyes wide with expectation.

"Rachel!" Mum had yelled. She rushed forward flinging her arms around my neck. It felt so good. I'd thought I'd never feel those arms again. Then Dad joined us and we were all in a tight hug, tears streaming down our faces. The lump in my throat was a good one this time, I finally felt safe, like maybe everything could be okay again. I just wanted to stay in their arms forever. They'd clutched me so tight I could barely breathe but I didn't care.

The police officer had quietly stepped out and left us together.

***

The door on our right opened and Mum and I looked up as Dad walked in. I'd sent him to find out about Rebecca. The police had told me she was here but I'd heard nothing more and my mind constantly ran from one terrifying scenario to another.

Dad's eyes were still red rimmed. I'd never seen him cry before.

"Well, I've found out she's okay but the doctors aren't saying much else at the moment," he said.

He knelt in front of me, his hands resting on my knees.

"The police told me a little more. Erm, that man …"

"The birth dad," I said. Dad nodded.

"Yes, your birth, erm, father. He'd filled the hole in."

My whole insides seemed to empty out, leaving nothing inside. I closed my eyes, poor Rebecca. And I'd left her.

"It seems that when he couldn't catch you, he decided to make sure Rebecca wasn't found. Who knows what was really going through his warped mind? There was an inner trapdoor, he'd closed that then filled the hole above with soil. Then he'd closed an upper trapdoor, covered it with earth and dry leaves then dragged a broken tree trunk across it."

My bottom lip trembled, guilt filling the void in me. "I shouldn't have left her."

"Then you would probably both have died." Dad spoke softly. "Rachel, if you hadn't brought help, they may not have found her until it was too late. She owes you her life."

I was shaking my head. He didn't understand. I was there, I saw that hole. I could imagine myself in it, picture the lid closing, the pitch dark, hearing the earth pound on top.

"I've got to see her!" Jumping up, the tea slopped, spilling onto the blue carpet. I'd forgotten I was even holding it.

"Rachel, you can't, Darling. Not yet." Mum touched my arm trying to reassure me but it didn't work.

I looked at her my need seeming to reach out through my eyes.

"Mum, I've got to see her." My breath caught as I grasped Mum's hand. "What if they're lying? What if she's dead?"

"Rachel, calm down." Dad's cheek bones were hollow. "This isn't helping. She's not dead, there's no reason for them to lie. We understand you want to see her and they'll let you in as soon as it's possible."

"No, you don't understand. You can't," I pushed. "Don't you see? Dad, Rebecca saved me! He was dragging me in when she grabbed his ankle and stopped him. We'd both be buried now if it wasn't for Becs. She saved my life and I ran away and left her. I should have helped her but I just ran and he buried her!"

I was gasping, trying to pull air into my lungs. Images of the night were flashing in my mind, images of Rebecca's face, my face staring up out of the hole and earth being thrown down on top. It was like one of those nightmares where you watch bad things happening to yourself but you're once removed and unable to do anything to save yourself.

"Darling, the police won't let you talk to her until they've got your statement," Mum tried. "We're supposed to wait here until they come. A social worker is on her way to have a chat with you as well, to make sure you're okay." She glanced at her watch, "I wish they'd hurry up so we can get you home for some sleep."

"I don't want to sleep and I don't want to talk to a social worker or the police. I won't believe she's alive until I've seen her!" I yelled.

I couldn't make them understand. The police had taken Rebecca out of the wood another way and brought me in the back of a police car. I'd been taken straight to A & E. A photographer had taken pictures of all my injuries. Doctors had examined me, took my blood pressure, cleaned up loads of grazes and bandaged my ankle but they wouldn't let me see Rebecca. They just said other doctors were looking after her. It was only after non stop pestering that my dad went to find out what he could. Until then he and Mum had clung to me like they were afraid I'd be snatched away again if they let go.

A nurse popped her head around the door.

"Is everything all right in here?" she asked, her eyes traveling from Dad to Mum before resting on me.

"I want to see my sister," I said. A new person, maybe she'd listen.

"I don't think …" she began.

"I want to see her!" Images of body bags filled my mind.

I could see by the looks they gave each other, they thought the captivity had unhinged me. Maybe they were right.

"I'll see what I can do," she said, a worried frown settling on her forehead.

I waited. Dad took the almost empty cup from me and Mum dabbed around with tissues. I'd really freaked them out. I couldn't rationally explain my feelings. Maybe me and Becs had bonded so much in that room that I couldn't bear to be separated from her. Maybe I just loved her now. Or did I think they were lying to me just as they'd lied about my adoption? I didn't know, I just had a desperate desire to see her, only then would I believe she was safe.

The nurse's head re-appeared.

"You can see her for a few minutes, but she has concussion so keep it brief and no exciting her."

Concussion? When did that happen?

I followed the nurse out of the room flanked by Mum and Dad. We followed the silvery-grey corridor to the end then turned right. Another long corridor stretched ahead and behind us, empty barring a couple of police officers further down and a nurse checking a clip board. Somewhere a baby was crying.

For a moment I wondered why it was so quiet, then remembered and felt my cheeks flush with embarrassment. It was still the middle of the night. Patients were trying to sleep and I'd probably just woken them all up.

One of the officers stepped towards me; it was the bulky one who'd first approached me on the road.

"Hello, Rachel. How are you feeling now?"

Wrecked, sprung to mind. I shrugged and looked at the door on my right.

"Your sister is in there," the officer said, following my gaze. "Now, Rachel, I must warn you. Your sister has concussion so we have not been able to take a statement from her yet. You can see her but not talk about what's been happening to you both. Do you understand?"

I nodded.

"Once you've seen her, we'll arrange for you to give your statement," he continued.

"Can't it wait until she's had some sleep?" Mum asked.

The officer shook his head. "I'm afraid not. The sooner we get the statement the more accurate it will be."

I looked at him. Rebecca was on the other side of that door and they were holding me up.

The officer nodded. "Yes, you can go in now."

"We'll wait here, Sweetheart."

It must have killed Mum to say that, but I was so grateful that she understood my need to see Rebecca alone.

I took hold of the door handle like it could break in my hand, opening it gently. Everybody said she was all right but I couldn't stop my stomach twisting as I stepped into the room. It only took a second to take in the computer in the far corner and the right hand wall covered in cupboards with purple doors. A stripy covered bed jutted out from a white alcove between the cupboards and in it, slightly propped up on pillows, lay Rebecca.

"Hey, you," Rebecca's voice was weak. "What took you so long?"

Her face was pale, nearly as white as the wall behind her and her eyes were half closed, but she was smiling at me. Warm relief washed through me like soothing oil. She was alive. Forget cups of tea, seeing Rebecca alive was all I needed. A drip stood at the side of her bed, feeding into the back of her left hand and a thick white pad was taped to the side of her head.

"What did he do to you?" I asked, ignoring the officer's instructions.

"Before he ran after you he tried kicking me again. I wasn't so quick that time. I don't remember anything after that until I woke up here. I hear I have you to thank for that." Her eyes, although tired, twinkled, just a bit.

"You don't remember what else he did?"

Rebecca shook her head then winced. If hearts and minds could smile, mine were grinning right then. She never saw the trapdoor shut. She didn't hear the earth fall on top. I walked closer and took her hand. It was warm but so thin.

"I'm glad you made it out," I said.

"I'm gladder," she said, her smile weak and eyes closing.

"I don't think you're supposed to fall asleep," I said, gently.

"Fat chance," she said, her eyes flickering open again, "With all the nurses in and out of here I'd have more chance falling asleep in the middle of Piccadilly Circus."

Suddenly aware something was missing I glanced around the room. "Where's your mum and dad?"

"Nurses kicked them out saying I needed some peace. I think they've gone for a smoke. But then someone around here made such a fuss they decided I could be disturbed just a bit longer."

I grimaced. "Sorry."

"No bother." She opened her brown eyes just a bit wider, looking intently up at me. "I'm glad you're okay, Rach."

"Me too," I agreed. "That you're okay, I mean," I added quickly. Rebecca smiled, her eyes already closing again.

"I'll see you later," I said, giving her hand a squeeze.

"Yeah," she said, sleepily.

Quietly I turned and left the room, looking back once more before closing the door. My twin was safe.

***

My reunion with Luke came the next day. He was round our house first thing.

Mum let him in and made herself scarce. Luke sort of shuffled into the lounge, his hands thrust deep into his jacket pockets.

"Are you okay?" he asked and looked at me for like, a nanosecond then his head dropped and his eyes focused on his spotless trainers.

I frowned, what was all this about? I'd expected an instant hugging session.

"I'm fine," I said, watching him and trying to read what I could see of his expression. "Don't mind the dressing gown, Mum's insisted on me relaxing all day. She won't hear of me getting dressed and makes me lie down every time she comes in the room."

I tried a little laugh, but it sounded fake even to me. "Are you okay?"

Luke's jaw worked.

"Look, I'm real sorry, Rach. It's my fault. I should've stopped him."

"He was too strong." Just thinking about that morning made my stomach flip over like a tossed pancake.

"But I do sports, I'm supposed to be strong. I'm your boyfriend, it's my job to keep you safe."

"That's not your job," I said, finally understanding what was wrong with him. "You're my boyfriend not my bodyguard."

Luke still hadn't lifted his head.

"I'll understand if you don't want to go out with me anymore."

199

I sat up, wrapping my dressing gown tighter around me.

"Luke, you really are a total idiot!" Now, that made him look up, a delicious frown on his forehead. "You're the hottest boy in school so of course I'm NEVER gonna break up with you. But if you don't come down here and give me a kiss I'm not gonna speak to you for a week!"

Maybe it was being kidnapped or spending all that time with Rebecca but eleven days ago I'd never have dared say anything like that! It had the desired effect. Luke's face split into a fantastic grin and he was on his knees beside me within a second. Then his lips met mine. His arms slipped around me and I wrapped mine around him. Electric warmth surged through me. I was in heaven, safe and feeling that nothing bad could ever happen again. My lips and his were definitely meant to be together, forever.

***

Mum kept me off school for the rest of the week. I think she was just scared to let me out of her sight what with Jed still being on the loose.

Eventually though, the third week in November, I stood shivering with Luke at my side, staring at the school gates.

"Nervous?" he asked, clouds of breath forming as he spoke.

I nodded.

"But not of Emma. It just feels weird, like it's a lifetime since I was last here. Like, I don't belong anymore."

Luke's arm tightened on my waist.

"Have you decided about changing schools?"

200

I shook my head. "I'm waiting until Becs comes out of the hospital. They're letting her out tomorrow."

Luke smiled. "That's great. Is she okay now?"

I smiled back. "Well, she's not totally right physically they say she needs more building up yet, but her mouth's back to normal. Since day two she's nagged them to let her go home and I think she's finally worn them down."

Luke grinned. "Yep, sounds like she's okay."

I turned back to the gates and took a deep breath. "Come on, let's get this over with."

I strode in with Luke attached to my hip. If I thought people had stared before it was nothing like they did now. Silence swept the school grounds as one after another spotted me.

"Come on." Luke whispered in my ear, leading me towards the doors.

"Hi, Rachel." A girl from my Math's class stepped in front of me. "Good to see you back."

Suddenly it was like a spell had been broken with everybody moving again, but towards me. Within seconds I was surrounded and plied with questions. It was weird, like I was a celebrity or something. I was real glad the police had told me not to say much as I'd have to testify in court once they caught Jed. It was a good excuse to say as little as I could until everybody was semi-satisfied and finally ebbed away. As the crowd thinned I spotted Emma, Carly and co, tight-lipped and glaring at me across the tarmac. Nothing had changed there then.

***

I visited Becs that night, as I had every night. She sat on her bed wearing jeans and white T-shirt like a queen surrounded by her subjects.

"Come in, come in!" She waved her hands and I joined her mum, dad and Liam at her bedside. "Have you heard? I'm getting out of here tomorrow!"

"Yeah, it's great news."

"I've got more …" Rebecca paused, her eyes glittering.

"Yeah?" I wondered what was coming, she looked way too mischievous.

"Mum and Dad are getting back together!"

Mrs Summers smiled. "We're giving it a go." She smiled at her husband who smiled back and I noticed her slip her hand into his.

"That's great!"

"And that's not all." Rebecca twinkled again.

"Go on?"

"They reckon now we've found each other we should have a chance to be closer. They've spotted a house just down the road from yours. We're moving in over the Christmas hols and I'll be going to your school in Jan!"

"Really?" This was fantastic. I'd have an extra ally against Emma and get to stay with Luke as well.

"Yep, really." She dropped back onto her pillow her major announcement delivered.

Things were definitely looking up.

***

Marcy stayed on for a few days before heading back to Scarborough to her job. It turns out she was the one who originally suggested the police check whether Jed had been released. After they said he had nothing to do with it she wouldn't believe it.

When he approached her, he said he'd keep us alive if she went back to him and while ever she behaved we'd be safe. She asked for evidence and planned to keep asking questions to make him keep his promise until the police could find us. As soon as he left her she rang the police and told them. The next night they tried to follow him but it seems he didn't entirely trust Marcy and had teamed up with the other white van owner. Somehow they did a switch mid journey so the police followed the right van but with the other guy driving it. Jed came to move us in the other vehicle. Another police team searched his house while he was out. They found no evidence of us but did find a letter that may have sparked off this whole kidnapping thing.

I talk to Marcy on the phone every week or so now and having heard what she did, even Rebecca's talked to her twice. It's still frosty between them but Marcy's thrilled just to be communicating. She goes to visit Mark occasionally but says she won't have him back when he gets out of prison.

***

Gran came up to ours as soon as I was home and stayed on for a couple of weeks. It was great seeing her again. She was back to her normal self, beating us all at scrabble by cheating. She told me and Rebecca we were too thin and proceeded to cook us loads of fatty, sugary foods which she insisted we eat even though we told her they weren't healthy. She said all the fruit she was giving us balanced that off. She tried getting liver and kidney down us as well but we drew the line at that one, although Luke lapped it up. Yuk!

***

Jed was caught early December. He'd taken off down south but the police found him. He confessed all, didn't have much choice really what with both me and Rebecca as witnesses. Not to mention the police finding Rebecca buried. He said he only intended to leave us there a few days until the police lost interest in him and he could find a better place. It turns out he'd put an air pipe, extra oxygen and loads of food and water in the hole, so maybe he was telling the truth. He said that after staying away for a few days he'd panicked when he saw how close the demolishers were getting and spent the whole of Sunday searching for a new location. I guess that's why he decided to make us pay that evening by tormenting us with the darts.

He'd bought all the supplies on Monday and made the trapdoors over two days. After extracting the evidence for Marcy on the Tuesday he went to the wood and dug the hole in the dark. The police said he seemed really proud of himself, bragging about how he'd managed to dig it all in one night without being discovered. He'd rested up on the Wednesday morning, given Marcy the evidence in the afternoon then come for us in the evening.

He told the police he'd not thought of doing anything until he got a letter a couple of months after he got out of prison. Now that he'd been caught and the police knew the part the letter had played in it all, they showed it to me and asked if I knew who'd written it. I sat on our settee with Mum and Dad on either side, reading over my shoulder. The writing was so familiar. It was like an itch right at the back of my brain but I couldn't quite get at it.

Dear Mr Phelps
You don't know me but I have heard about you and would like to help you. I'm sure you would like to re-unite your family and I am able to help with that.
Your wife, Marcy is living in Scarborough and she is now in touch with

your twin daughters. One is called Rebecca
Summers and she lives in Swinton. The
other, Rachel Brooks lives in Rotherham
(address enclosed). I have also enclosed a
photograph taken from a local paper. She
is standing with her adoptive mother who
has recently had a book published.

Mr Phelps, I feel that what
happened to you is totally unjust and your
family do not deserve such a wonderful
husband and father. However, I am sure
that if you can get together with them you
will be able to convince them of your
intentions.

I wish you well with your reunion.
Yours sincerely
(A concerned friend)

My whole insides twisted, bile rising in my
throat. I'd managed to scratch the itch.

"Emma Samuels," I said. I couldn't believe it.
Emma had caused all the trouble. The letter was dated
the day after Mum's article appeared in the paper, so all
the time her cronies were wheedling and twisting, this
letter was already on its way to Jed. She'd wanted him
to find us, to hurt us. It didn't matter what Luke
decided, she'd already set the wheels in motion.

I just sat there shaking my head, my hand over
my mouth.

"Do you know where she lives?" The burly
officer asked.

"Oh, yes." It was hard to keep the loathing out
of my voice. "I'll give you her address right now."

And I did.

***

Six months later Jed was sent down for ten years for kidnap and actual bodily harm. The jury bought his defense that he never intended to kill us and would have returned us to our families in time. I'm not sure that I'll ever believe it but at least we don't have to worry about him for a long time.

When the conviction was final, I asked a special favour from the police and they agreed. The next day, with Luke and Becs on either side of me, I pinned a copy of the letter in Emma's hand writing onto a notice board in the school hallway.

"What's that then, Brooks?" Carly scoffed, with Emma, Louise and co, just behind her.

I turned and looked at Emma. Her face had lost every drop of colour as she stared at the piece of paper.

"Where did you get that?" Her words were barely more than a whisper.

"The police gave it to me as a keepsake," I said, fixing my gaze on her wide eyes. "You've finally made a mistake."

"It's nothing to do with me," she tried.

"Looks like your writing," Carly said, stepping forwards for a closer look.

Emma stood there twitching, looking left, then right, then back at me like she wanted to run but keep face at the same time. A small crowd had gathered around us. They blocked the hall, watching and listening, slight murmurs flitting between them.

Carly had been quietly reading the letter but turned at last to Emma.

"You Witch!" she spat. "That's the most evil thing I've ever seen!"

Her outburst brought a universal gasp.

"I didn't write it!" Emma denied, "Rachel set this up, she's trying to make me look bad."

"Well she doesn't have to try hard," Rebecca muttered.

"Shut up you, you're just the copy. You should've stayed missing, both of you!" Emma snarled.

Curious, the spectators edged forwards in small groups, read the letter then turned accusing eyes on Emma.

"It's your writing, Emma, I'd know it anywhere," Louise looked at her friend as if seeing her for the first time. "I can't believe you did that, they could've died."

"How was I supposed to know what he'd do?" Emma spat, then suddenly realised she'd all but confessed.

"Check mate," Luke said, a satisfied smile on his face.

"Our stupid printer!" Her chin jutted out. "It never works. I keep telling Dad to get rid of it!"

"Should've printed it at school," I said, unable to stop my lips spreading into a smile.

Emma's eyes narrowed. "Oh yeah, and have everybody see me do it." She paused. "Why did the idiot keep it? He should've burnt it or something."

"Because, that's what he is, a crazy idiot, who's locked up now, where he belongs." A warm glow burned inside my chest; finally Emma looked as nervous as I'd felt all year.

Emma's twitching stopped, her hands clenched. She looked like she'd turned to stone. Her eyes seared into mine, asking how I could have beaten her. For the first time ever, everybody was glaring at her.

She left school the next day and never returned.

Already aware of Emma's part in it all because of the police's visit to her house, I heard her parents decided to home school her. Her dad finally saw the true nature of his daughter and I heard he became really strict after that.

I just hope Emma learns and changes for the better as a result, but who knows?

Carly stayed at school. She stopped bullying. She'd no choice really. Everybody knew how she teamed up with Emma and if ever she tried to threaten somebody at least three other people stood up for them. She's still not the friendliest person in the world but she's getting better.

***

I still have nightmares about those days in that dusty room. Whenever I pass a boarded up house my chest gets real tight and I walk on quickly, looking the other way. For months Mum, Dad and Luke wouldn't let me go anywhere alone. They insisted on driving me around or if walking I had to be on the inside away from the road. I didn't mind. Every time I heard a vehicle pull up near me I'd hold my breath and every nerve would send shards of ice through my skin. They still do. Although I go out alone sometimes now, I carry a personal alarm. If any man comes too close I clutch it like a hand grenade ready to activate it instantly if needed.

Sometimes I still cry. Sometimes me and Becs cry together. Our counselor says it'll take time for all of us.

***

Me and Luke are closer than ever. I don't know about the future but after all we've been through I think we're gonna stick together. He still makes electric currents run through my body every time he touches me and he even misses football practice sometimes just to walk me home. Now that can't be bad!

Me, Mum and Dad are getting on great. I finally figured out that being adopted doesn't matter at all. Just the looks on their faces when they came to the hospital that night told me everything. They were both so thin with black rings under their eyes, but their faces lit up like fireworks when they saw me.

I understand now that they love me and know that's all that matters.

THE END

Acknowledgements

Thank you to my proof readers for your constructive feedback, Pam for your adult view point, Ellen from Swinton Community School and Hania from Rawmarsh Community School for your teenage perspective. Thanks also to Cornerstones Literary Consultancy for your editorial guidance.

Thanks to the gentleman walking his Alsatian who helped me find my way out of Melton Woods. My research visit would have been much longer than planned without your help!

Thanks also to Heather Akroyd, Hazel Brand and the staff of Doncaster Royal Infirmary Children's Ward for arranging my visit and supplying lots of useful information.

Thanks to everyone who reads my books and recommends them to others, without you my readership would be much smaller. Thanks also to Waterstones, Newstyme and Rotherham Library Service for supporting me.

Thanks especially to YouWriteOn.com and FeedARead.com without whom this book would not exist.

Watch out for:

Time Fixers

By Gail Jones

Jess is a feisty agony aunt for her friends at
school, but when mysterious Eli arrives and
invites her to be part of a futurist agency has
Jess taken on more than she can handle?

The overseers watch history and send young
people to help their peers avoid decisions which
will destroy theirs or others lives.

Jess has no idea how challenging this will be or
how much danger she is going to face.

Time Fixers
The start of a new series.

coming soon

To Keep up with all the latest news:

Visit Gail's website:

www.gailjonesbooks.co.uk

Or check out her facebook page:

www.facebook.com/GailJonesbooksUK

Or follow her on twitter

www.twitter.com/gjonesfiction

Lightning Source UK Ltd.
Milton Keynes UK
UKOW051536140612

194392UK00001B/13/P

9 781781 763520